"Dresses are what you buy a mistress," she reproved, but his blood surged at the capitulation in her voice.

He smiled. "Oh, *mistress.* That's such an old-fashioned concept. It's time it was put to bed."

"Don't use that sexy tone with me." Her attempt at sounding stern didn't quite come off. Not with that husky, breathless quality in her voice. "Haven't I made it clear? I'm still an old-fashioned girl and I *haven't* come as your mistress. Or to be put to bed. I'm here as your sounding board, remember? Your executive assistant."

"And it's as my EA that I'll be escorting you to that cocktail party. And it's as your *boss* that I insist on attiring you in a manner befitting Martin Place Investments."

As a child, **ANNA CLEARY** loved reading so much that during the midnight hours she was forced to read with a flightlight under the bedcovers, to lull the suspicions of her sleep-obsessed parents. From an early age she dreamed of writing her own books. She saw herself in a stone cottage by the sea, wearing a velvet smoking jacket and sipping sherry, like Somerset Maugham.

In real life she became a schoolteacher, and her greatest pleasure was teaching children to write beautiful stories.

A little while ago she and one of her friends made a pact to each write the first chapter of a romance novel on their holidays. From writing her very first line Anna was hooked, and she gave up teaching to become a full-time writer. She now lives in Queensland, with a deeply sensitive and intelligent cat. She prefers champagne to sherry, and loves music, books, four-legged people, trees, movies and restaurants.

DO NOT DISTURB

ANNA CLEARY

~P.S. I'M PREGNANT! ~

Harlequin®

TORONTO NEW YORK LONDON
AMSTERDAM PARIS SYDNEY HAMBURG
STOCKHOLM ATHENS TOKYO MILAN MADRID
PRAGUE WARSAW BUDAPEST AUCKLAND

Recycling programs
for this product may
not exist in your area.

ISBN-13: 978-0-373-52820-2

DO NOT DISTURB

First North American Publication 2011

DO NOT DISTURB

For my lovely niece, Linda.

CHAPTER ONE

THE tall, dark-haired guy in the suit strode into the meeting room of Martin Place Investments, and the hum of conversation faded into silence.

Mirandi Summers sat straight in her chair, her pulse-rate a little elevated. Everyone else was in black or shades of grey. She hoped her violet dress wasn't too pretty for the office.

'Morning,' Joe Sinclair said without bothering to glance at his assembled market analysts, too concerned with checking the hardware for his presentation.

'Morning, Joe.' The responses came from around the room, some bright and eager to please, others more subdued.

This morning Joe looked authoritative and slightly on edge, something in his manner creating more than the usual tension. How he'd changed in ten years. Hard to imagine him burning up the bitumen on his bike now.

'Ah, here we go.' The boyish grin that had the temps drooling made a brief appearance on his lean, tanned face, then vanished.

A brilliant, multi-coloured graph illuminated the screen. On it a number of spiky criss-crossing lines curved upwards, shooting towards infinity.

'There now. Look at that.' Joe's cool blue eyes grew sharp and focused, a line creasing the space between his brows. 'You see before you the future. Looks good, doesn't it?' He sent a commanding glance around at his employees and Mirandi joined the chorus of assent. 'And it *will* be good, people, I think I can promise you that. It will, but only if we are willing to learn from the mistakes of the past.'

He frowned and pulled a face. 'Tomorrow, as you know, I'll be flying off to this conference in Europe. Before I leave I want to know everyone has a clear view of the factors influencing MPI's current direction.'

He touched the button again and another graph lit the screen, this one's projections not quite so sunny. He swept the faces of listeners. 'I'm keen to hear your ideas. Can anyone suggest—'

Suddenly he stopped in mid-sentence. His frown deepening, he swung around until his acute blue glance lighted on Mirandi at the end of the row.

'Oh—er…Miss Summers. *You're* here. Are you—intending to stay?'

Mirandi felt something grab in her insides. Under the weight of her red hair her nape grew uncomfortably warm. 'Well, yes. Of course.' She glanced about her. All the other market analysts were assembled, their laptops at the ready. 'This is the future projections meeting, isn't it?'

Joe Sinclair gave his ear a meditative rub. 'Yes, it is. Just that I was under the impression—Ryan had mentioned something he wanted you to do this morning. Didn't I hear you say that, Ryan?'

Beside Mirandi Ryan Patterson stirred himself to attention. 'Oh, did I? Yeah. Yeah, that's right, Joe. Sorry, Mirandi. I forgot to mention the Trevor file.'

Mirandi gave a small, gurgling laugh. 'Oh, the *Trevor* file. Now that's a mistake from the past if ever there was one.' Everyone joined in her light-hearted laugh, including Ryan Patterson. Everyone except Joe Sinclair, that was. His black lashes were lowered, as it it pained him to look at her.

Smarting, Mirandi changed position slightly and crossed

her legs. 'As it happens, Joe, I've reconciled the Trevor file. It's all finished and accounted for.'

There was a moment of stunned silence, then the other analysts burst into a round of surprised applause and congratulations. Mirandi couldn't help but feel gratified. The Trevor file was notorious and had been around for a long time. Perfect material for a new MA to cut her teeth on. Especially if the boss needed something to keep her occupied whilst keeping her at a distance.

Joe smiled too, though Mirandi felt his quick smouldering glance leave a trail of sparks down her legs. 'Have you, now? Slick work. But have you written the letters to old Trevor and his sons to let them know the outcome?'

Mirandi's flush climbed higher, but she said in dulcet tones, 'Well, as you know, Joe, Ryan's assistant will be back next week and I suspect *she'd* like to have that pleasure.'

Beneath his lashes, Joe's half-lidded glance lasered Mirandi from across the room, though he said with silky gentleness, 'I don't think you understand quite how we operate here, Miss Summers. Until those letters are in the mail the file is incomplete. I'm sure you don't want to leave unfinished business for others to deal with.'

Mirandi felt a savage jump in her blood pressure, though she controlled it, surrendering to the command and rising from her chair with cool grace. 'Unfinished business?' She threw him a mocking smile. 'Heaven forbid. What would you know about that, Joe?'

She made a point of giving Ryan and the others a cheeky grin and a wave, then swept from the room, feeling a visceral flash from Joe's eyes sear through the fabric of her dress.

As she strode back to her desk along the corridor his voice drifted after her. 'Are you free to give us your attention *now*, Ryan?'

It took her a couple of hours to get over the latest clash, but she cooled down in time. She was determined not to go home with tears in her eyes this night. In fact, she might have managed to forget all about it by the end of the day if Ryan Patterson hadn't found something else for her to do. *Might*.

But he had, and ironically here she was, in the middle of the afternoon, approaching no-woman's land. Joseph Sinclair's private residence.

Twenty-second floor. Apartment four.

Leave the folders on the table in the foyer where Joe can easily find them, and hotfoot it straight back to work in time for the three o'clock credit review, were Ryan's spoken instructions. Unspoken, but lurking under the surface like crocodiles, was his more crucial advice. Don't linger there hoping for a chance to flirt, sweetheart. Forget leaving any traces of yourself behind to intrigue him. No strands of your flaming red hair or whiffs of your perfume, strategically squirted here and there. He's no good for the likes of you. He'd use you up without a second thought and break you in the process.

As if Mirandi didn't know that already. She had personal experience. If eyes were the windows to the soul, the colour of Joe Sinclair's was a liar. That heavenly blue had already lured her in once only to leave her floundering, and she wasn't a kid of eighteen any more, naive and willing to be enchanted by a charming young rebel with nothing to lose and everything to prove.

She couldn't have been persuaded to set foot in Joe's posh apartment building if her entire floor hadn't been overstretched with preparations for his big junket to France, and no one else available.

2204. Mirandi paused before the imposing door. Funny how even with a legitimate card key in her hand she felt that prickle of intruder's guilt. Noiselessly, the lock flashed green, she walked in and…

Whoosh.

Oh, wow. The light. The space. And through those double doors into the spacious sitting room—the views.

So this was who he was now. Of course, if an outlaw's natural brilliance had skyrocketed him up the corporate ladder to the highest echelon in an investment firm, why wouldn't he live in a palace at eye level with the top of the Sydney Harbour Bridge?

Hypnotised by the grandeur, she stepped through the double doors, still clutching the folders, and tiptoed the couple of miles across Joe Sinclair's satin hardwood floor to gaze out through the glass. Sydney looked like the postcards from this height, all blue sea, sparkling rooftops and scrapers under a bright azure sky.

She turned and cast an awed eye over the joint, inhaling deeply to soak in the atmosphere. It smelled rich. The furnishings were spare, but tasteful. Mahogany and leather, a richly-hued oriental rug, a couple of paintings…

This glossy apartment was a million miles from that two-roomed flat, their favourite trysting place all those long ago summer afternoons where Joe had initiated her into the delights of passion.

Her eye fell on a photo, frozen in time inside a glass prism. It showed a decrepit motorbike leaning against a wall. It was Joe's old motorbike, before he'd rescued it from rust and made it shine. His pride and joy.

Regret for that long ago summer welled up in her, and, like the sentimental fool she was, even while she smiled in remembrance tears misted her eyes. For a minute she was back in the magic time, the summer she turned eighteen.

It had been late spring, for the jacarandas were in flower, purple carpets underfoot all over Lavender Bay. As sweet and glowing in her mind as if it had been yesterday she was there, standing under the spreading boughs of the jacaranda in the churchyard after morning service, fresh out of school and in love after one brief, world-shaking encounter. There she was, dreamily listening to Auntie Mim chat with friends while her father, who was Captain of the Lavender Bay chapter of the Christian Army, was still engaged in farewelling his flock at the church door.

She could still see her old love-struck self. Nodding, smiling, pretending to listen, holding her secret clutched to her heart until her romantic radar, newly alert, pricked up its ears at the approach of a motorcycle.

A wild hope bloomed inside her, and she swung around just as the big bike roared into the paved entrance and skidded to a halt, its racket idling down to a low, predatory growl.

Astride the mean machine was Jake Sinclair's wayward son, Joe, looking long, lean and darkly satanic as his cool blue gaze combed the little clusters of friends and families in their Sunday uniforms and pastels. Black jeans outlined his powerful thighs, while a black leather vest left his bronzed, sinewy arms bare and highlighted the glossy raven black of his hair and two-day beard.

'What's *he* doing here?' Auntie Mim frowned. 'What could he be wanting?'

Though Mirandi had often noticed him about—who among the females of Lavender Bay hadn't?—she'd only spoken to him for the first time the day before when he'd helped her retrieve her books from a puddle outside the library.

After years of steeping herself in romantic sagas and grand passions played out on the Yorkshire moors, Mirandi knew instinctively what he wanted. *Who.* And to her intense and terrified joy, his bold blue gaze lit on her with an electric summons that sizzled across the paved churchyard and straight to her ovaries.

She was gripped with the purest excitement she'd ever experienced. For a second she vacillated. On the one hand there were her friends, her father, Auntie Mim, the entire church gathering, and on the other the bad boy on the big bike.

Then Joe Sinclair cocked his handsome head at her and

grinned. A primitive urge as deep and irresistible as a cosmic force blazed to life inside her. She took a step in his direction, faltered, took another step, then, thrusting her hymnal into Auntie Mim's grasp, so as not to worry the innocent woman, breathed, 'Auntie, I think I can guess. He's in search of salvation.'

Then she walked across the yard.

'Well, hello, Joe,' she said, every inch the pastor's gracious daughter, though her excited pulse was effervescing through her veins like raspberry fizz. 'Why don't you come in and join us?'

Joe Sinclair flicked a glance across the goggling congregation, then his black lashes made a sleepy descent over his smiling gaze. 'Or you could come for a ride.'

This was only the second time she'd had a chance to dwell on his face up close for any length of time, and she couldn't take her eyes off him. He had a strong straight nose, sexy, chiselled mouth and jaw and gorgeous cheekbones. He was all lean, hard and angular, except for his black lashes. They were amazingly long and luxuriant, but in a masculine way that caught at her lungs and melted her very bone marrow.

'Oh…' she faltered, plunged into a dilemma '…I don't think… Well, my friends are all… And there's—there's my auntie…'

He broke into a grin then that illuminated his lean face and made him so handsome her insides curled over. 'I haven't come for your auntie.'

She didn't hesitate very much longer. With a hasty, placatory wave at Mim, she climbed onto the passenger seat, tucked her skirt primly around her knees, let her fingers sink into his lean ribs and was swept away on the most exhilarating ride of her life.

Oh, it had been thrilling. Clinging to Joe on the bike was the closest intimate contact she'd ever had with a raw, vibrant man.

And, unbelievably for a lanky girl with red hair and no boyfriend experience—hardly even a first kiss to boast of, unless she counted Stewart Beale and a clumsy pash at the school dance—he'd taken her back to his flat and kissed her until her insides melted like dark chocolate and her brain turned to mush.

Then he'd gently but firmly unbuttoned her modest little blouse with his beautiful lean hands and stroked her breasts until she trembled with a delicious fever. And *then* he'd unzipped her Sunday skirt, and with artful, virile skill had demonstrated things to her about riding she'd only ever read about in trashy magazines.

Oh, it had been a golden time. Joe was cynical and mocking about serious things like church, but tender and affectionate with her. He didn't mock her when she tootled her recorder on Saturday mornings in the mall with the church band, though she felt so self-conscious she frowned the whole time so as not to be tempted to laugh.

Every day with him was an adventure. He made her listen to songs, *really* listen, and in between his university studies and part-time work introduced her to writers and ideas she'd never before encountered.

He was passionate about music, rock especially, and animals, and could be so enchanted by the beauty of a wren or a honey-eater he would make her stand still for minutes so as not to scare it.

She could still hear his voice, urging her to take her time. 'Look,' he'd say. 'Look *properly*.' Joe's mother was a painter, he'd once told her, and had taught him how to really look at birds and natural things from when he was a tiny little boy. And he was an artist himself of a sort. Once in the flat she stumbled on some poems he'd composed. Vivid little pictures painted in just a few bright words.

She was supposed to be enrolling in uni, but how could she concentrate on such mundane stuff as her future when she was intoxicated with love? So she deferred her enrolment, and told Auntie Mim and her father she needed a gap year to experience life.

Mim was unimpressed. 'He'll never amount to anything. He's nothing but trouble, that lad. Why can't you find some nice, steady boy from the church?' She'd have been surprised to learn he could find beauty in simple things. That often when Mirandi was in danger of pushing the limits of recklessness too far, it was Joe's steadying hand that restrained her.

When he wasn't fixing up motors he took Mirandi fishing in his father's old dinghy in the little estuary at the head of the bay. How she remembered those lazy afternoons, drifting in the boat, dreaming about the future. Joe in his ancient blue tee shirt that reeked faintly of machine oil no matter how often it was washed.

And she'd loved him. Oh, how she'd loved him.

Shame it had all had to end so miserably. But she'd learned from it. As the song said, life was a bittersweet symphony. And after she'd lost him, once she was over the heartbreak, she'd come to the realisation her happiness depended on herself and not another person. Every woman was a goddess in her own right and was honour bound to walk like one.

She cast a wry glance around at the glossy apartment. Did that mocking, irreverent, irreligious Joe Sinclair still exist somewhere, deep down under the layers of his Italian suits and the corporate skin he now inhabited? Or was this new sophisticated Joe the animal he'd truly been all along?

She paused at an antique sideboard, where a crystal decanter stood among a selection of lethal-looking bottles. A few familiar labels. Whisky, gin, and there was the vodka, her old favourite and first acquaintance with the evil stuff. She could have laughed to think of herself then. How easily she'd succumbed in the name of sophistication. Anything to impress her lover, who'd been so worldly-wise in her naive eyes. Older by a whole six years, though way older in the hard lessons of grief and loss.

She could imagine what her father would think of it all. After a lifetime of caring for the homeless and manning the city soup kitchens, he wouldn't be any more impressed than he'd been ten years ago when he'd scraped Joe's father off the pavement and driven him home because he'd gambled his last dollar and couldn't afford the bus.

It popped into her head that if Joe knew she was here now, invading his private domain, he'd have every right to be furious.

She was conscious then of a vague sensation she hadn't experienced since a time in her childhood when her father had inadvertently left her alone in the house while he rushed to tend some distressed person. A reckless, almost irresistible desire to make the most of her freedom and do something wicked, like raid the freezer for ice cream.

Not, of course, that she'd do anything like that *now*.

However, with Joe ensconced in meetings with the board for the rest of the afternoon, along with Stella, his EA, surely there was time for a little tour of appreciation?

CHAPTER TWO

Joe Sinclair directed his long stride back towards his chief executive office, then on an impulse made a left swerve and took the lift down, loosening his tie. Would the day never end?

Something was wrong with him.

If it wasn't weird enough to have been tossing and turning in his sleep these past weeks like a criminal with a conscience, now he had developed the disease most fatal to bankers.

Astonishing this could happen to *him*, a guy with a gift for finance, but in the last couple of months—ever since the casino development had been floated, in fact—board meetings had become excruciating. When had the musical chink of money flowing into the coffers of Martin Place Investment started to fall so flat?

He nearly had to pinch himself. Wasn't he the guy who'd pursued his career with such single-minded zeal his colleagues called him the Money Machine? Nothing ever interfered with his core business. No distraction, no interest, no woman. All of his passions lived in their separate compartments and life was a velvet ride. No collisions, no dramas.

Down in the street, he breathed the open air and lifted his face to the afternoon sun. His first time AWOL in years, he considered how best to make the most of his stolen afternoon. In the absence of a helicopter to lift him out of the business world and drop him somewhere clean and pure, like

Antarctica—or what remained of it—he tossed up between a gym and a bar, and the bar won.

Not for the alcohol, per se, so much as the possibility of finding some luscious lovely decorating the venue with a view to entertainment.

One who didn't want to buy him. He tried not to think of Kirsty, his sometime lover. Way back then those first few weeks had been amusing, but now...

Now, a familiar feeling of ennui lurked around the edges of her carefully groomed image. He could tell, the signs had been there for weeks, an unpleasant crunch was looming. Her father's offer of the house in Vaucluse and an honorary directorship had been the clincher. Every one of his instincts was shouting at him to run like hell before the prison gates clanged shut.

Ironic, wasn't it, that these days society guys wanted to buy him for their daughters? *Him.* Jake Sinclair's son. One-time rebel and seducer of innocent virgins. Did he really come across now as the sort of guy who would trade his soul for connections?

Between them they'd tried every trick in the book. Kirsty had even attempted to make him jealous, flaunting some silver-tailed Romeo in front of his eyes to make him care. What she didn't know—what each of his women had to learn—was that Joe Sinclair didn't have a jealous bone in his body.

He paused at the entrance to the Bamboo Bar, then strolled into its dim, cool refuge and ordered a Scotch. The lunch crowd had diminished. A couple of leggy women perched on barstools glanced his way, but instead of welcoming the signals he was swept with a wave of weariness.

Suddenly it all seemed so predictable, the conquest dance. He'd advance, they'd retreat. He'd advance a little further, they'd take a flirty step in his direction. He'd play it cool, they'd come on strong... It was all too easy.

But, God, he *loved* meeting women. What was wrong with him? He must be sick.

He should be feeling upbeat. Here he was at the top of his game, the world his own personal pomegranate. Tomorrow he'd be flying to the south of France. A change of scene, the possibility of picking up some new contacts, useful information from some of the masters of the game before he decided whether or not the firm should risk its shirt on the Darling Point casino project.

So why should his heart sink at the prospect? Good old reliable Stella would be along to smooth the way and attend to all the little details of his comfort. Well, most of them. And Stella was—well, she was risk free.

Unlike some.

An apparition reared in his mind, one that burned in his thoughts a time too often, in fact, for a highly disciplined CEO with responsibilities.

Was it a whole five weeks since HR had floated her name before him as the potential candidate for the new Market Analyst position the firm was creating? His first reaction had been incredulity. A more unlikely MA he couldn't imagine. Why had she applied? Was she hoping to glean some advantage from their past acquaintance? Had she forgotten how things had played out?

Mirandi Summers, his one-time squeeze. His first instinct was to give her the thumbs down. Last thing he ever wanted was to revisit that final scene where betrayal hung acrid in the air like smoke after a massacre. So why hadn't he blocked her application?

It wasn't guilt, exactly. He'd done the right thing in the end, hadn't he? The *only* thing. He could hardly believe he was still wasting his time even thinking about it.

All right, so these days she wasn't quite the shy, sweet little honey who'd tied his guts in knots. She'd grown up. Her green eyes had acquired the glitter of experience. Where once they'd reflected every passing emotion with honest fervour, these days they were guarded. Wary. But in the competitive jungle of office politics—a girl like her...

The bad taste this morning's meeting had left returned to him with full force. Why the hell was she so keen to swim with the sharks? If only she knew it, he was trying his best to protect her. Given half a chance some of those others would cut her to shreds.

He ran a finger round the inside of his collar. How could he ever be expected to concentrate with her in the room like a woman-sized pack of dynamite?

It had been the same since the day she started. That first morning when he'd strolled down to the coffee room and she'd wafted into view his lungs had gone into cardiac arrest.

Old memories, old guilts had rushed to the surface, and for a guy as fit as himself his blood pressure had made a surprising leap. He'd had to close his eyes a second to reorient himself.

She still radiated the same animal vigour that had sucked him in and driven him wild in his twenties, but now her leggy, coltish beauty had matured into sensuous, smooth-flowing curves and long, silken limbs that had rocked through him like a warm, sultry samba. Limbs he'd once enjoyed to the utmost draped around his neck.

Her bright hair showed none of its old tendency to curl. Now it hung smooth and silky down her back. But surely that purple dress she'd worn today was a little snug? He could see what other guys would make of her. *Hot.*

He was seized with a maniacal desire to rush across the room and drag some covering around her.

As usual, just thinking of the womanly handful she'd become lit a dangerous simmer in his blood. Clearly, hiring her had been a mistake. He'd arranged for her to be tucked under Ryan Patterson's wing for a few weeks while Patterson's EA was on leave, just so she could at least find her feet before she was thrown in with the pack, but it didn't help Joe Sinclair's problem one bit. She was a burr in his imagination. In the end, unless he could work her out of his system, nothing else for it, he'd have to sack her.

Not that he gave a damn about her now, one way or the other. Although, all right, he had taken the time to check out her personnel file just for interest's sake.

She still lived in Lavender Bay not far from the old neighbourhood, and still not married, apparently. Surprising really, considering the course her old man had mapped out for her.

His mouth tightened in a grimace, though the insult had long since ceased to sting. Hell, if he'd been her father he'd probably have done the same thing. She'd been so soft, so tender and giving. Malleable. Too malleable to be at the mercy of a villain like himself. He should probably thank the old guy. It was probably the insulting lack of faith in all things Sinclair that had spurred him on to show the captain and the rest of Lavender Bay that he could rise to any height he set his mind on.

But as for Mirandi in this world...he still couldn't get over it. Did she have any idea of some of the cutthroat decisions she'd have to make? Perfectly good, useful projects she'd have to reject in favour of other, more lucrative investments? The hearts she'd have to break? She was as suitable for the job as a baby. Hell, with her upbringing, if she had any idea of what the board was contemplating at this very minute her tender conscience would send her running in the other direction.

Once or twice he'd been unable to resist an impulse to stroll by Patterson's office. Just to check she was settling in. He'd caught a few glimpses of her, once frowning in concentration at her desk, another time chatting on the phone. To a client, he hoped. She looked perfectly relaxed and confident, though sometimes people had no idea they were struggling and in need of help.

The last time he'd given into that impulse he'd caught her

laughing at something Ryan Patterson said, and she'd glanced around and spotted *him* strolling by. Instantly her laugh had died and her face had assumed that cool, mysterious façade that could drive a man crazy.

He was used to his employees behaving with caution when he was around, it came with the territory, but sometimes he couldn't help wishing he'd gone easier with her on her first day.

He'd resisted checking on her after that, but knowing she was there, her honeyed temptation fragrancing the air along there—the same air breathed by *Patterson*—flavoured every minute of his every day. In fact, he wondered now if it had been such a good idea awarding Patterson the pleasure of easing her in.

He'd chosen the guy because Patterson was mild and well liked, but the choice might have backfired.

If only the bloke would stop raving about her abilities as if she were his own personal discovery. It wasn't beyond the bounds of probability he was in *lust* with her, if a pale, blond milksop of a guy could conjure up enough red blood cells to experience anything so turbulent.

Joe was no stranger to turbulence. Even during his recent bout of disturbed nights, those times when he was torn from his sleep in a cold sweat, as if in search of further punishment his mind had immediately turned to her. How she looked, her expression on her first day in the job when he'd been forced to show her her place.

There'd been something in her face. Ridiculously, it brought back to him with violent force the stricken look he'd seen in her eyes that last time she'd come to his flat. How vulnerable she'd been back then. He'd seen something like that look again this morning.

He tried to suppress a familiar twinge in his guts. It wasn't guilt, exactly, it was just…

He *must* be sick.

His phone buzzed, and he saw it was Stella. He considered letting it ring through to the recorded message, then his conscience got the better of him.

'Stella?' As crisp as ever. Mrs Efficiency would never guess he was standing in a bar room, Scotch in hand, contemplating bolting to the ends of the earth.

Unusually for her she sounded agitated. 'Oh, Joe, I'm on my way to the hospital. It's Mike, my youngest. He's been in a bike accident and they've put him in intensive care. I'm sorry, but I have to be there.'

Bloody hell. *All* he needed. But he said, 'Of course, Stella. Take all the time you need.'

'They're talking about operating. I'm afraid I won't be able to accompany you to Monaco, after all. I'm so sorry.'

'Forget about it,' he said, wincing. 'It can't be helped. Stay with your son. That's where you're needed most.'

'Oh, thank you, Joe. Thanks for being so understanding. And don't worry about your airport transfers. Those have all been taken care of. When you land in Zurich all you have to do is…' Instructions, instructions, instructions. 'And I've left the hotel confirmation on your desk. Don't forget to…' More instructions, more tedious details. It was a wonder she didn't offer to pack for him. A further round of abject apologies and medical details, then the anxious mother disconnected.

Despite his annoyance he felt a surge of approval towards his executive assistant. She'd been touchingly excited about the trip, in her restrained way. A woman prepared to make such a sacrifice for the sake of a son old enough to fend for himself was admirable. Rare, in his experience.

His mood darkened. As if it weren't already a bore, now it would be ten times worse. The long flight by himself, airport queues. Delays. Fights over taxis. Crowded beaches. French food, French people. Days of being locked inside conference rooms with hundreds of eager delegates from around the globe all blathering on about the fabulous weather. As if there weren't enough weather right here in Sydney.

He'd have to dredge up his rusty French. Why the hell couldn't they have held the thing somewhere cold, like Switzerland or Helsinki? Investment bankers could discuss the casino industry quite as well in those places as on the Côte d'Azur.

The very thought of the place sent a wave of distaste through him. He gave himself a mental shake. This was so unlike Joe Sinclair, mover and shaker in high finance, he had to wonder if he was coming down with flu.

Sighing, he flicked open his phone and dialled the office number. No use fighting it. He was a prisoner of his own success and there was no escape.

'Get me Tonia in HR.' He waited. 'Ah, Tonia—Joe. Look, Tonia, take a look through the lists and see if you can find someone who can be spared to fill in for Stella on the trip, will you?' She chatted for a moment, then he slid the phone into his jacket pocket.

Someone pleasant, he should have added. Someone interesting who could keep his mind off the dark places. With a fatalistic shrug he tossed off his Scotch and set down his glass, then, ignoring the lovelies at the bar, walked out into the street.

He reminded himself he was a lucky guy. Someone would turn up.

Mirandi began to relax a little on her prowl around Joe Sinclair's apartment, though she restricted herself to merely glancing into most of the rooms for fear of shedding DNA.

Curiously, there were no other photos. Not a sign of attachment to a single living soul, though she knew he'd never keep any pictures of his family. Joe had always been tight-lipped about them, but Auntie Mim knew the story. His mother had walked out when Joe was a boy of nine or ten, and his father, who'd been a talented architect, had spiralled into an addiction and gambled away all his assets, including the house, over his son's head. The very home he'd designed and built with his own hands.

Joe had never liked being reminded of those times even when she knew him, so what had she expected to see here in his new life? That late-afternoon shot of him and her at the beach, grinning into the camera as though their hearts beat as one? Or any one of that string of girls she'd seen clinging to the back of the old Ducati?

Afterwards. When he was grinding her into the dust with his indifference. Lucky the violence of her youthful passions had been burned out of her.

Through a partly open doorway she glimpsed what must be a bedroom, and hesitated. She shouldn't. She really shouldn't. Though maybe it would help her develop some deeper understanding of how her old love was travelling now.

Her old love. Listen to herself. The truth about that had come out, plain for all to see, so why waste her time peering down that shady lane? She doubted she'd have taken this job at all if she'd realised at the interview that the Joseph Sinclair, CEO of Martin Place Investments, was in fact her old boyfriend, Joe. That final parting had been—so cruel.

Still, she had to be fair and remind herself Joe never knew what it was she'd come to tell him that day. Remembering the moment no longer had the power to make her flinch with anguish, but it was burned into her bone marrow.

His blue eyes, bright with that strangely fierce intensity. 'It's over,' he'd said, his voice hoarse. '*We're* over.' And when in her total shock and devastation she'd whimpered a question, his savage, 'Go home, little girl. Run back to your daddy.'

As break-ups went, it had topped the memorable list and left track marks on her soul. And while time might have cauterised the wound, running into him her first morning in the coffee room had done more than just shake her up. At first glimpse of him, even after ten years the things he'd said had come hissing back and aroused echoes of the old emotions.

The instant she'd caught sight of him a violent upheaval had rearranged her insides, though *he* hadn't seemed similarly affected. His long, lithe stride had checked for less than a heartbeat, and he'd strolled across to her with all the cool, confident composure of the boss man.

She had to remind herself she was no one special. Just someone he'd met along the way. A chick from the past.

His blue gaze flicked over her, veiled, appraising. 'Well, well. Mirandi. Hi.'

So cool. While she was all at sea. His eyes, his deep voice, and her lungs paralysed. No oxygen, no floor under her feet. And straight away, the scent of him. Some woodsy cologne evoking cleanliness and masculinity in the old familiar rush.

As she took in the immediacy of his dark, lean sexiness her gap year came spinning back and she was that giddy girl again, thrilled and half-terrified to be singled out by the bad boy with the wild reputation. Held breathless once again in his heart-stopping blue gaze, she had to restrain an impulse to touch him.

A thousand impressions assaulted her. He was just as devastating in his city suit as he'd been in denim and leather, though at thirty-five his handsomeness had settled into harsher lines.

Sterner. More defined. Every inch the high-powered executive. She wondered how many people here besides herself knew that underneath his designer and beautifully laundered fine white cotton shirt a heavy-duty tattoo rippled down his arm. Even thinking about those arms could still bring her out in a sweat.

Was it so surprising then that her heart, her flesh, her emotions all surged in joyful remembrance? When she saw him her heart was thundering so loudly she could barely hear herself speak.

'*Joe*. Hello.' Straight up, that husky little catch in her voice. 'How are you? I—got such a surprise when I found out you were the CEO here.'

His expressive black brows twitched as if he didn't quite believe her. 'You didn't know?'

'Oh, well, I mean, I knew it was *a* Joseph Sinclair, but I didn't know it was *m*—the Joe Sinclair I once knew.'

His eyes veiled and their last goodbye opened between them like a wound. But he shrugged and gave that faintly mocking smile she knew so well. Used to know.

'Hard to believe?'

'Gosh no, of course not. But—with no photo of you on the website, for some reason—I visualised a much older person. You know the type. Bald, plump…' She made a roundish outline with her hands. 'Toadish. Cigar in breast pocket.' She gave a nervous laugh, aware she was talking too much, and her desperate phrases grew jerky. 'Not the…person I used to know. It was only that I—knew the name it seemed like a—a sign, you know. An omen. Fate, or something.'

Heaven help her, *finally* she managed to draw breath.

'Well, that explains it,' he said smoothly.

She flushed, realising with chagrin how deeply she'd exposed her insecurity. Surely after ten years the past should have lost its sting. But she couldn't help herself, because all the while things she'd once known so well about him were striking her afresh, sucking her in in the same old way.

He didn't often make direct eye contact, and just like before she found herself waiting, breathless, for every glance he flashed her from beneath his black brows. And like before, those blue glances had the power to sear through her entrails and leave a powerful impression, like some rare piercing glimpse of a kingfisher's wing.

He'd pierced her with one of them right then. But it was an

ironic glance, one that revealed nothing of the warmth he'd once shown her. Before the break-up, that was. Before she'd wrecked things by offering her eternal love.

'Would you have started here if you'd known?' he said.

'I—of course I would,' she lied. 'Why not?' She'd managed an artificial smile then to conceal her pulse. But though she'd kept her voice steady, she knew her redhead's skin was betraying her as always, lighting her up like the Macquarie beacon with every minuscule fluctuation in her emotions.

'Why not indeed?' There was a faintly sardonic inflection in his tone that recalled the rejection as if it were yesterday.

She retreated from that horror, hurrying into a safer direction. 'Oh, and, er, do you know how long it will take before my own office is ready? At the interview I had the impression that the position was all ready to go. I appreciate Ryan mentoring me for a few days, of course, but I'm pretty keen to get started on my real work. Forge my own direction, so to speak.'

She gave a small laugh but he didn't join in. In fact, his brows drew together in disapproval. 'I think you'll find that working with Ryan will show you the ropes twice as fast as you could learn them on your own.'

'Oh, I'm sure. Though I am quite a fast learner.'

His black lashes flickered infinitesimally. 'I remember.'

A silence fell. Nerve-racking seconds ticked by that grew excruciating.

Why had she said that? She racked her brains for something warm to say that would ease the tension. 'You know, Joe, I've often thought of you—since… Wondered—how you were.' She smiled, nearly put out her hand to touch him, but, jarred by the flicker in his cool blue gaze, controlled the impulse.

There was a definite warning in that glinting glance. *Don't go there*, it read, as stern and uncompromising as if it had been emblazoned in official lettering.

What a fool she was. Of course he didn't want to be reminded of his past, not here in this austere place surrounded by his employees. Realising she'd opened herself up to another rejection, she flushed outright then and her speech died, hanging her out to dry at the critical moment.

He stood frowning while her discomfort mounted, then he said, 'Look, Mirandi. You're here on probation, same as any new employee. I hope you understand that any personal history between us is of no relevance. All that matters here is how well you perform your job.'

Her insides jolted as if she'd stumbled blindly into a rock face. In a wave of mortification it occurred to her he might think she had hopes of him again. That she might have taken the job with a view to reviving their old connection.

Perhaps he read her embarrassment, for his tone softened a little. 'To be brutally honest, I'm surprised to see you here. Investment banking is a tough world to survive in. I'm not sure this work will suit someone of your temperament.'

'My—temperament?' came from her dry throat.

'Well…' He hesitated, then scratching his ear, said, 'I think you'll find that in finance an excess of emotion and, er, sensibility are luxuries we can't afford.'

She bristled all over. Sensibility indeed. Did he think she was still that gormless idiot who'd broken her heart over him a thousand years ago?

Lucky she was of a proud disposition and could think on her feet while being eviscerated.

'Oh,' she said, 'please don't worry about me, Joe. I've toughened up. Every night I sleep on a bed of nails.' She spread her arms. 'Go on. Dish it out. I can take it.'

A muscle twitched in his gorgeous jaw, then he said drily, 'Very dramatic. I suggest you pour all that *passion* into your work.' There was slight inflection in the way he said the word that reminded her he was no stranger to its various applications.

For a minute or perhaps an hour or two his blue gaze

seemed to burn through her face, then he snapped out of it and looked at his watch. Brisk, unemotional Joe Sinclair, CEO.

'Right. Ryan Patterson will be reporting on how you perform, so since we keep strict hours here you'd better drink your coffee. Oh, and, er…good luck.'

With a curt gesture he walked away.

So brusque. So—unwelcoming.

Indignation threatened to overcome her. So she had an emotional side. She was human, wasn't she? He hadn't seemed to object to her passionate nature ten years ago. She stared after him, striding through the department like an autocrat. She could hardly recognise the guy. If he hadn't still been oozing hotness she'd have wondered if she'd been talking to his twin. Anyone would think he'd been born with a briefcase in his hand.

She smarted for minutes over the implication that she was too soft for the business world. Too *weak*. On what had he based that assessment?

Her credentials were all there in her CV. Her years in the bank, the promotions she'd earned. Just as soon as her office was ready and she could start her own work, she'd show him how efficient she could be.

She could have done with a few private moments to give her galloping pulse time to settle, but she noticed Patterson's curious gaze follow Joe then shift to her, and she knew she had to glide on like a goddess and act as though nothing had happened.

Standing here now in his apartment, searching for some lingering essence of the lazy, laughing, teasing Joe she used to know, she wondered how she could still be so affected by him. Time should have done its work by now. She was a mature woman, hardly that green girl who'd worshipped him and been his adoring slave.

She supposed running into him again had dragged it all up again in her mind. The truth was, she'd never experienced anything like the intensity of the passion she'd had for him. Although at the time, during all the months of grieving, Auntie Mim had made the observation that Joe wouldn't have given her up so abruptly if it hadn't been purely about the sex.

Mim had been right about some of it. There was no denying she'd been followed by a string of wild little hussies, as Mim had termed Joe's other girlfriends. Hot chicks. Even so, she could never regret her wild time with him. Joining the chicks. How could she, when it had been the most exciting time of her life? The time she'd felt most alive.

Perhaps that was why gazing into his bedroom now exerted a violent fascination, though her conscience was telling her loud and clear that a man's bedroom—especially a boss's—an *ex-lover's*—was his fortress. Or should be.

Sadly, while her scruples tried to assert themselves, her feet in their four inch heels were itching to push that door wide and cross the forbidden threshold, and before she was half aware of it she was *in*, staring at a rather severe four-poster heaped with pillows and richly draped in luxurious brocaded fabrics.

Oh, yes. The master suite.

Somehow Joe's bed made her awash with sensations, not all of them positive. Its decadent appeal was amplified by its reflections in several long mirrors.

How would it feel to lie in there at night with him? Her pulse quickened as she imagined his handsome dark head on those champagne satin pillows. They looked soft enough, but looks could be so deceiving where pillows were concerned. For herself, she preferred hers *very* soft, though as she recalled the younger Joe had never worried about anything so domestic.

A simple mattress on the floor, those green patterned sheets—that had been their passion bed, the candle shedding its glow into the small hours on their entwined bodies Joe's concession to romance.

She stared at the four-poster, then, on an impulse, sat on the edge and slipped off her shoes. She dragged a pillow into position, then gingerly lay her head on it. After a moment she lifted her feet onto the bed, then stretched out and, involuntarily relaxing, released a long and languorous sigh.

Ah-h-h. She let herself sink into the bed's soft, sensuous and at the same time buoyant embrace, her head cradled by one of the softest, most delicious pillows she'd ever experienced.

Oh, the comfort. Fearful at first of letting herself go, she lay still a moment, imagining herself floating on a cloud. Perhaps it was inevitable, given her experiences with Joe Sinclair, but her thoughts started to drift down a certain illicit alleyway. One she'd fought and struggled to avoid ever since the coffee-room encounter.

Imagine, for example, it was midnight. Suppose Joe arrived home unexpectedly and found her here?

Her blood warmed to the scenario. For all his powerful six-three Joe was a quiet guy. He never raised his voice when gutting someone with a few well chosen words, and he seemed capable of walking as silently as a cat when prowling the corridors at work. It wasn't impossible to imagine he might walk in and catch her unawares.

Almost unconsciously, she changed position to arrange herself more voluptuously, like Goya's painting of 'The Naked Maja', though of course she didn't take her clothes off. Her little fantastical indulgence was only for a second. She closed her eyes, picturing the scene.

He'd come in, find her here, and be overcome with the old desire. He'd take off his tie and slowly unbutton his shirt…

How well she remembered his beautiful chest and hard, muscled abdomen. Even in his Armani suit it was clear he still looked after his athletic frame. Perhaps he worked out in a gym. There was probably one in this very building.

Although… Shouldn't they start with a kiss? After so long she wouldn't enjoy being rushed.

She banished the undressing scene and started afresh. He'd come in and catch her here, and be so overwhelmed by desire he'd swoop onto the bed beside her, take her in his arms and kiss her with deep, romantic passion. Forget that it was a bit like the Sleeping Beauty or Goldilocks, or whoever. Those babes wouldn't have known how to savour the kiss, anyway, whereas *she*…

Her lids sprang open. Was that sound from inside the apartment, or something next door? The pipes, perhaps? She strained her ears for seconds, then, hearing only silence, relaxed back into the fantasy.

The kiss. No, it was annoying, but before she could really enjoy kissing him she would need some sort of discussion about what had happened. Why he'd suddenly become so cold and unapproachable at the time she'd most needed him.

Why he'd changed overnight from her tender, teasing lover into that grim, distant stranger. Though, on the other hand, recriminations about the past at that exact point could destroy the magic.

So. First he'd kiss her and caress her, and then he'd say…

An instant later a surprised growl jolted her back to earth and she looked up to meet Joe Sinclair's stunned, incredulous gaze. He was standing in the doorway in the lean, solid flesh, staring at her as if she were an hallucination.

CHAPTER THREE

TRANSFIXED INTO A SORT of paralysis, he was holding a phone glued to his ear.

Mirandi scrambled off the bed and made a useless attempt to smooth the coverlet.

'Oh, *Joe*. I didn't expect… I was just…' She noticed the folders on the floor where they'd fallen. She stooped to snatch them up, conscious of the burning tide of sheer mortification rising through her limbs and chest and turning her face red hot.

But she hadn't lived through the past ten years without acquiring a few life skills. Faced with total humiliation, with her back to the wall, Mirandi Summers could schmoozle her way out of a situation as well as the next woman.

Drawing herself up to her full five-seven, she met Joe Sinclair's bemused gaze with resolve. 'I think you should know you have a mouse problem.'

His black brows twitched. A glint lit the deep blue of his irises.

Without taking his gaze off her, he shot a few words down the phone. 'It's no one. I'll talk to you later.' With a deliberate calm, he snapped the phone shut and slipped it inside the jacket of his sleek suit. It buzzed again, but he cut it off and directed the full force of his stunning gaze at her.

'Ah,' he said. 'Mirandi.'

It had always thrilled her that for a guy of such few words,

ANNA CLEARY   35

his voice had a deep, rich, almost musical quality. Eighty per cent cocoa, the rest pure cream. But something in the tone of that little exclamation, something smooth and satisfied, as if he'd always suspected she was dying to crawl back into his bed any way she could, and now he was proven *right*, roused an indignant spark in her.

Forget that from her current vantage point he was tall, with his big athletic frame easily able to block a doorway. She'd been towered over by him before, perhaps not with him having the power of life and death over her job, so to speak, but the situation had occurred, as her body seemed vibrantly aware.

She eased into her shoes, grateful for the added inches, then thrust the folders into his hands. 'I was asked to deliver these.'

'To my bedroom?

'Of course not, Joe. Absolutely not. I intended to put them on the table in the foyer, but when I opened the door and I saw the mouse… I—must have disturbed it. I didn't think you'd want to have to deal with *that* when you got home, so naturally I—took off after it.' She gave an uncertain laugh he didn't join in with, then glanced about her and gave her most convincing shudder. 'It's in here somewhere.'

'In my bed, presumably.'

She felt her flush deepen, especially when she noticed him make a familiar, scorching inventory of her curves. Some things never changed.

His mouth had always been so stirringly expressive. As though sculpted by some sure celestial force, his lips were firm and masculine, the upper one narrow, the lower one fuller, the whole stern ensemble promising the ultimate in sensual pleasure. And delivering, as her body now yearningly recalled.

'Well, it ran—in here, yes. I lost sight of it and… Well, I got scared it might run at *me*. So I'm afraid I—had to jump up on the, er…' A hollow in the pillows was glaringly the size and shape of her head. 'It may not still be in here right *now*, of course.' She tried for her most earnest expression. 'I'm sorry. I didn't have time to think out a strategy.'

'You seem to be doing quite well now, though.'

She evaded his sceptical glance, her face afire just when she needed it to be cool. All right, so her story was thin and he didn't believe a word. He didn't look half as furious as he should be. Warning bells were clanging in her head. It was a situational rerun. Joe, Mirandi, *bed*.

Fantasy may be one thing, reality was definitely another.

'Anyway,' she said, marshalling some faux briskness, 'I have to get back to work.' She made a move to walk past him, nerve-rackingly conscious this was a sackable offence and she'd handed him a platinum-plated advantage in the male/female adversarial stakes.

At the last possible instant he stood aside to allow her through, to her intense relief, though at the moment of passing closest by him the intense masculinity radiating from him singed the skin cells on that side of her body to the third degree.

As she escaped into the hallway and made for the sitting room other phones started ringing, though the sound was cut off almost at once.

'I can't talk *now*, Kirsty,' she heard him say, the merest hint of irritation in his voice. He raised it a little. 'Hold it there, Mirandi. Just a minute.'

He caught up with her just as she was scurrying across an enormous Persian rug towards the front door, faster even than the mouse. If there had truly been a mouse, that was.

'Don't go. Stay a minute. I want to—talk to you.'

He didn't touch her, but it was as if an invisible arm had reached out and grabbed her by the scruff. There was no resisting. She turned to face him, eye to eye, and since he was the one asking her embarrassment over being caught subsided a little. She gave a stiff nod.

'Sit down.' He indicated a handsome chesterfield with

deep cushions. His black lashes flickered. 'Can I get you a drink?'

'No, thanks.' She allowed herself the glimmer of a smile. 'I'm working, aren't I?'

He smiled, raising his eyebrows, and she had a sudden vivid flashback to her vodka afternoon. The first time she'd succumbed and broken her pledge. After that, her solemn childhood promises had fallen thick and fast. Enslaved by her sexual sorcerer, she'd have drunk hemlock if she'd thought it would make her his equal in sophistication.

To her relief he didn't allude to her youthful indiscretions. He strolled over to his drinks sideboard. 'Do you mind…?'

She shook her head, gestured for him to go right ahead. She was the last person to dictate to others after her spectacular fall from grace.

He poured himself a whisky. 'Sit, sit.' He waved his hand in an autocratic gesture, directing her towards the sofa, and she made the wary concession of perching on the edge.

He dropped into a chair across from her, leaning forward a little, his long, lean fingers wrapped idly around his glass. Fingers that had once been familiar with every curve and hollow of her body.

She faced him, her old partner in crime. In passion.

'So…do you feel—settled into the firm?' His glance sank deep, and she could feel the old pull. That magnetic attraction that sparked up her blood and made her heart quicken with excitement. So dangerous, so addictive.

She felt his gaze drift over her, flick to her legs, and her sexual triggers responded with shameless willingness. Even after everything, something inside her switched on to preen and revel in his appreciation.

She shrugged. 'I'm settling in. Everything seems to be going well enough, I suppose, though to be honest I wish I could spend more time on my own work.' She glanced at him from under her lashes. 'I'm really looking forward to my own office.'

'Ah, yes.' His eyes veiled. 'How's it going with Patterson? Helping you find your feet?'

'Oh, yeah.' She nodded, smiling to herself as she thought of Ryan's wry words of advice on everything a girl needed to know on how to survive at Martin Place Investments. 'Ryan's been fantastic. Nothing's too much trouble for him.'

Beneath his black lashes his eyes glinted. 'Fantastic. Tell me about you. How's life?'

Did he mean at work, or personally? She doubted he'd be interested in her father's health situation. Her social life, perhaps? Ah, no. She got it now. None of the above. Long after their year of living dangerously, he wanted to know if she had a partner. A lover.

'Things are fine with me,' she said. 'Splendid.'

'Splendid?' He lifted his brows.

'Absolutely.' Well, she was hardly likely to tell him she hadn't been very successful in that regard. That she'd noticed in herself a regrettable tendency not to be able to hold onto a boyfriend. Possibly because she found it quite hard to open up. Her legendary passion must have been letting her down. Curiously, for one of her renowned temperament, they found her too—self-contained. Inhibited, one had complained.

'Anyway, I finished my degree and—'

His eyes glinted. 'Yeah, I'm sure I read that. Well done.'

She flicked him a narrow glance. Was he mocking her? At the time she'd known him he was juggling several part time jobs so he could pursue his ambitions, while she deferred her own education, reluctant to tear herself away from him, greatly to her family's concern.

How they'd stressed over it. The nagging she'd endured.

'Where did you say you studied?'

'Brisbane.'

He lifted his shoulders in sardonic amusement. 'As far away as possible from Joe Sinclair.'

'No, not at all,' she said, flushing, though of course it was true. 'That was the best course of its kind available at the time. Anyway, it was after the...*after* we—broke up.' She mumbled the last few words.

'Not long after, though,' he dropped in, searching her face.

'No.' A nerve jumped deep in her visceral region. He was sailing close to home. Someone should warn him to take care. There were things he wouldn't want to know.

There was a jagged pause, then she said, 'Well, anyway, I decided science as a lead-in to medicine wasn't for me after all and found the job in the bank. It was only ever meant to be temporary, but to my surprise I found I had quite an aptitude for it.'

His brows edged together. 'For finance?'

She nodded, wishing he didn't have to look so dubious.

'What's your plan?' he said. 'Your ultimate goal?'

'Careerwise?'

'Of course. What else?'

She gave him a wry look. What else indeed?

'Oh, well,' she said glibly, as if she weren't a twenty-eight-year-old woman with twenty-eight-year-old eggs in her ovaries. 'I'm aiming for the stars. Managing Director of a firm like this one would seem like a good jumping-off point.'

His sexy mouth twitched and she realised with some irritation he felt amused by her grand, audacious vision. Possibly his masculine ego felt challenged.

'Anyway, as I said,' she finished, 'I'm doing fine, or I will be once I can flex my muscles. What about you, Joe? I can see you've arrived.' She swept an admiring glance around her. 'This is quite—breathtaking. Not bad for a boy who was expelled from two high schools.'

He sipped his Scotch. 'Not quite what your family would have expected, I dare say.'

She put on her bland, non-committal face. Mim certainly hadn't expected him to do well. A solid pillar of the church, she'd made her feelings crystal clear on the subject of that wild heathen Joe Sinclair at every opportunity. Her father hadn't had so much to say, possibly because he was in the dark about her mad love affair, dreamily going about the business of caring for people, never knowing his beloved daughter had plunged in to navigate the treacherous reefs of passion without a compass.

Aware of having pushed her close to a raw edge, Joe lowered his lashes, careful not to glance too long at her breasts, though it was a wrench. His eyes drifted to her mouth. Was she wearing lipstick? Her lips had always been naturally rosy, plump and ripe as cherries, and sweet. Sweet and fresh, like none he'd tasted since.

His mouth watered with a sudden yearning and he realised he was being ridiculous. Of course she'd tasted sweet. She'd been *young*, as the captain was so quick to point out, as he, Joe, had been himself. It was highly unlikely she'd still have that effect on him. Though it would be interesting to find out.

'You *look* very well,' he said, smiling, his pulse quickening with the stir in his blood. 'Still live with your old man?'

Mirandi felt his glance sear her. 'Not for a long time.' Their eyes clashed, then disconnected as if some electrical collision had thrown out sparks.

'Ah,' he said. The chiselled lines of his mouth compressed. He gazed consideringly into his drink, his black lashes screening his eyes, then he said, 'Was it hard to make that break?'

'Everyone has to do it sooner or later. Grow up.'

A silence fell. The air in the room tautened while the wounds between them flared into life.

His eyes scanned her face. 'And have you? Grown up?'

She shrugged. She'd learned enough about love and its

consequences. 'What's there to say? I'm older now. I know better. How about you?'

'Older.'

His mouth edged up at the corners in that sexy way he had and she felt herself slide further towards some cliff's edge. How could someone so bad for her still be so appealing?

He pierced her with one of those glances. 'Do you have someone in your life?'

His tone was casual, as if he didn't care one way or the other. But there was a stillness in him, as if all at once the world turned on her reply.

She relaxed back in the sofa and crossed her legs. 'Is this something bosses need to know about their employees, Joe?'

He smiled at the small challenge. 'Bosses are only human. Isn't it natural to be curious about old lovers?'

She felt an internal flinch at the word, but he'd used it deliberately. *Lovers.* Surely they were people who loved you and wanted to keep you? Especially when you were scared to death?

He continued to taunt her with silken ruthlessness. 'I'd have thought you'd be married by now to some solid citizen in the suburbs. Some pious, clean-living guy who plays the church organ. Mows the grass on Sunday. Takes the kids to the park.'

She felt a sudden upsurge of anger, but controlled it. 'Is that where you're headed, Joe?'

'Me? You've got to be kidding. You know me better than that.'

'Yes,' she said shortly. 'I remember well.' She conquered the emotions unfurling in her chest. After all, it had been ten years. 'Anyway, would that life be so wrong?'

His eyes were mocking, sensual. 'It might be. For you.'

'Oh.' She expelled an exasperated breath, but no doubt his assumption was her own fault. It had been her fatal mistake.

She'd worked so hard to convince him she was super-cool and fearless and ready to fly, when all along she'd been this weak, clinging little girl who'd slipped on the most elementary of rules for conducting an affair with a bad boy. Not any more, though. 'What makes you an authority on what's right for me, Joe?'

He said, deliberately tweaking her tender spots, 'Knowing you in your formative years. Don't tell me you've forgotten your walk on the wild side.'

If only she could. A complex mixture of emotions rose in her, regret and anger uppermost, but she crushed them down and gave a careless shrug, though it pained her to dismiss the enchanted time and its bitter aftermath.

He smiled his devil's smile. 'Remember the time you borrowed your old man's car? How many girls can claim they swam naked at Coogee at midnight, then drove home in their dad's car?' He added softly, 'Still naked?' He broke into a laugh. 'That was some ride. If Captain Summers could have seen his little girl that night.' His voice softened. 'You were—ablaze.'

Straight away her mind flew to the inevitable postscript to that wild, exhilarating ride. His flat. His hard, bronzed beauty in the flickering candlelight, in startling contrast to her own pale nudity. The excitement of being held in those muscled arms. Her passion for him, the intense heat of their coupling…

She met his eyes and knew he was remembering it too. Despite herself she felt the stirrings of desire, tightening the air between them, the sudden sweet possibility of sex. What could be more likely, with the two of them in this otherwise empty apartment? Her breasts swelled with heat and suddenly she was awash with the old bittersweet sensations. The yearning, the helplessness.

How easy it was for a man. No consequences, no griefs to bury.

But she'd already made those mistakes. She said steadily, 'Look, much as I'd love to stay and reminisce, I have to go. I have a job, remember?' She made a move to get up but he put out one lean hand.

'No, don't go. Please. Patterson won't be worried. You can tell him I waylaid you for my own wicked purposes.' He smiled, a sexy smile that crept into her and coiled itself cosily around her insides, as if he shared some secret with her. Some private, *intimate* secret.

The trouble was, he did.

She examined her fingernails. Oh, heavens. Here she went, sliding down the serpent again in the old snake-and-ladders game of life. Was she imagining it, or was the mood seductive? Who else had ever been able to look at her with quite that degree of sexy assurance, as if they knew it was only a matter of time before she fell into his hands like a ripe plum?

She supposed her small test of his pillow had fuelled the flames. Why on earth had she succumbed to such an idiotic impulse? Whatever he was about to suggest, dinner and conversation or an afternoon of dalliance, a glimpse back at all the old pain and humiliation was enough to resolve her.

With a big firm *no* crystallising on her tongue, she looked up again and shouldn't have. He was examining her, one corner of his mouth edged up in a half smile, his stunning eyes gleaming with an amused comprehension that rushed through her like a fizzy drink, stirring her to her entrails.

Was this the time to lose her nerve and turn respectable? No other man had ever been able to look at her like that, as if he knew all the secrets of her sinful heart. Heaven forgive her, but just this once, whatever decadent scenario he suggested, shouldn't she at least listen?

But he surprised her. 'To be honest, I'm glad we have this chance to talk. I guess there are things we both need to acknowledge before we can move on.'

She moistened her lips. Was this how he operated now? He

bamboozled women into his bed? 'Move on? Move on where? I'm not sure I follow…'

His brows edged together. 'Well…' He shook his head, then started again. 'We've come up against each other again, and…' He gestured with his hands. 'It's an opportunity to set the record straight. I know I for one can look back at that time on things I'm not comfortable with. Wouldn't you prefer to operate from a basis of truth?'

If she hadn't been seated she'd have been rocked off her stilettos. What was he doing? Inviting her to be honest? Demanding that all pretences be dropped?

What planet was he on?

The phone rang again. Joe made no move to answer it, instead continuing to search her face with his compelling gaze. He started to speak again, earnestly, sincerely. 'Meeting you again has made me…reevaluate. Some of the things that were said back then… The *way* things happened, have had a—an afterlife.'

He met her eyes with such honesty she felt a deep surge of response. Her heart quickened, suddenly brimming with long-buried emotions. Hope, tenderness, the faint stirring of that all too weakening love. Despite all her protective barriers every cell of her being started urging her to listen to what he was saying.

Maybe there truly was a time when lovers could speak to each other without artifice. Open their hearts. Maybe she should have told him the simple truth that last time they met. Given him his chance to be a hero. Maybe if he understood what had driven her to lower her guard, humiliate herself like that, *beg*…

The phone clicked to answering machine and an urgent female voice flooded the room. 'Joe, I know you're there. *Don't* hang up, please.' Despite an attempt at lightness the voice croaked slightly on the don't. 'We really need to talk.'

He sprang up and grabbed the phone.

'Sorry, Kirsty,' he said in a low voice, 'I'm occupied right now. I'll call you back.' He was about to hang up but something his caller said arrested him and he listened. Even from where she was sitting, Mirandi could hear the agitated female voice, beseeching.

If only the woman had been able to see him she wouldn't have persisted. He was frowning, shaking his head, every line of his body from his chiselled, sensuous mouth to his long, lean limbs set in a steely, definite *no*.

'No. I didn't promise that,' he said coolly. 'I've never said anything *like* that.'

Mirandi's heart started to thump out an unpleasant drum roll. Wasn't this the old familiar scene? How well she knew the female part, having played it herself. The more emotional and extravagant the distressed woman, the cooler, more controlled and inaccessible the man. All that female emotion. So inconvenient.

That impulsive moment when she'd actually flirted with the possibility of opening up her heart to Joe Sinclair died. Thank heavens she hadn't. Embarrassed about intruding any further into his private life, she stood up and started to edge towards the door. But catching sight of her, he held up his hand.

'No, stay there.' His gaze locked with hers and he said quietly, 'Please.' Then he walked away into another room to deal with his call.

She stood there on tenterhooks. Should she stay, or should she go and end this intriguing and unlikely conversation, in which it sounded as if Joe was actually prepared to open up and give his take on their past relationship? Though she could see how risky it would be, with the potential emotional fallout. Still, the temptation to stay and hear what he had to say was tantalising, to say the least.

She truly wasn't straining her ears, but every so often she couldn't help overhearing snatches of his conversation from the study.

'I'm not…why I have to explain…' His voice had taken on an ominous crispness. '*Business*, pure and… As it happens my assistant isn't— Oh? Why's that?' He gave a harsh laugh. 'Certainly I do… Well, I wouldn't expect her to sleep on the street.' After an extended silence, she heard his voice again. 'That's not how I want to play it, Kirsty.' Another silence, then, 'Well, if that's… I think you're probably right… Yep… Yeah…for the best.'

There was something very final in those last few phrases. Mirandi might be an absolute fool at understanding men, but she could tell when one was cutting a woman loose. And she could remember how it felt.

Looked as if poor Kirsty had crossed the line, just as she had ten years ago. Was Kirsty in the same situation? Begging him to know how he felt. *If* he felt.

She felt a wave of disillusionment. For a minute there he'd almost had her convinced. The more things changed…

Inside his study Joe dropped the phone with an angry grimace. The sheer enormity of the woman, attempting to dictate terms to him now about the trip. He wondered, not for the first time, if her father had put her up to it. The fact that the old man had a seat on the MPI board… Could the old manipulator have enlisted his daughter as a means of keeping a check on Joe's meetings in Monaco?

Fuming, he was about to call the devious old devil when the phone rang again. He snatched it up, ready to deliver a few sharp words, but this time it wasn't Kirsty.

'Oh, Joe.' Tonia's voice purred down the phone, and he relaxed and allowed the anger to drain out of him. 'About Stella's replacement—what about that new girl, Mirandi? Her office still hasn't been decided and Ryan's EA comes back next week, anyway.'

'No, no, Tonia. Not possible.' Hell, that *would* open a can of worms.

Although… Would it necessarily?

'Ah-h-h… Leave it with me,' he said quickly. 'I'll think about it and get back to you.'

He replaced the phone very gently in its cradle. No, no, no. He couldn't do it. Out of the question. Though…well, certainly it would provide a neat system solution. He could see the appeal from Tonia's point of view. Business in the office would tick over as usual without anyone being disturbed.

But it was far too dangerous. Fraught with risk. Dynamite in what it could unleash. Possibilities flashed through his mind, some of them quite scintillating, but he thrust those away. No rational man would ever open that door again.

Still…

He felt his pulse quicken.

Why not? Those old issues from the past were over and done with now. He could contain the situation, keep it on an even keel. He'd always been able to control it. Come to think of it…maybe this was the very thing needed to defuse the past and its grip on his imagination.

He flexed his shoulders, then strolled out to the sitting room in time to catch her in the act of sneaking to the door.

'Hey. Now, don't run away,' he said. 'There's something I need to ask you. Oh, and—sorry about that interruption.'

Mirandi surrendered her escape bid and turned to examine him with curiosity. Was she imagining it, or was there an added bounce to his step? His eyes were alight with positivity. She felt a bitter pang. Was this what finishing with a woman did for him? Smiling, brisk Joseph Sinclair, CEO? In charge, his lean, tanned hands clean, with no clinging traces of the woman he'd just dusted off?

He hesitated a second, searching her face.

'Do you have a current passport?' When she nodded his eyes lit with satisfaction.

'Great. I'm needing an assistant for my trip to France and it might as well be you.'

'*Me?*' Stunned, she took a second to collect herself. 'Are you kidding? I mean… Isn't Stella going?'

'She can't come. Her son's been in an accident and she needs to be with him.' He brushed all that aside in a gesture. 'So? I need an assistant. Can you be ready by noon tomorrow?'

She searched his face for signs of derangement. Could he be serious? Had he forgotten who she was?

But no, he was back to behaving like the office Joe, crisp and businesslike, focused and professional. Trouble was, with her emotional deeps still in disturbance, her sexual sensors in a spin from the Joe she'd been with a few minutes earlier, the whole world felt as if it were spinning too fast. What about the cool head she'd sworn to hang onto from now on?

'Well,' she dithered. 'But…but what about Ryan?'

'Ryan? Oh, forget *Ryan.*' He gave the name an inflection, as if there were something wrong with Ryan. 'Leave him to me. I'll fix Ryan. So?' He advanced on her, smiling, his masculine assurance so attractive, persuasive. She caught the scent of him, that faint appealing tang of soap and sandalwood. 'It'll only be a few days on the Riviera.'

While her senses responded to Joe-Sinclair-induced sensations, her giddy head whirled with visions of charming seaside resorts, villages and little bays with fishing boats tied up in their marinas. For an instant visions swayed in her mind of the two of them together, swimming in the Mediterranean, lazing side by side on golden sands.

'Oh, gosh,' she said weakly. 'The Riviera does sound— *lovely.*'

'You think?' To her surprise he gave a small grimace. 'Yeah. Well, I admit the possibilities are improving.' His voice deepened the tiniest fraction, and his glance flickered over her with a sudden mesmeric gleam that made her catch her breath. There'd be the hotel, of course. Her mind shied away from that risky image.

He strode into his study and came back with a thin sheaf of papers and a laptop, murmuring something about flights.

Visions shimmered in her mind. Surely he wouldn't be suggesting she go unless he was planning it as some sort of interlude. Though warning bells clanged from some distant horizon, part of her was warming to the notion of a French fling with her old lover. How thoroughly sophisticated. How *delicious*. And why not? She was an adult, wasn't she? She could handle it.

Temptation trickled along her veins like silky honey. She could see the movie version now. *Rapprochement on the Côte D'Azur*. Nothing so sexy had come her way in years, though of course there were dangers involved.

As she eyed his handsome, assured face frowning into his screen she reminded herself of how weak she'd been with him in the past. Putty in his hands. Her eye fell on the smooth, bronzed, clever hands that had broken her heart.

Could she really betray her younger self like that? All the pain she'd suffered, her sad little loss? The trouble was, gorgeous though he might be, the beloved object of her passionate young heart, Kirsty's call rang fresh in her ears. And what about those other women, the chicks who'd come after her?

Regrettably, reality fastened its grip on her and shook her wandering brain cells back into place. 'I don't think so, Joe.'

He glanced up from his screen. 'What?'

She placed her hand on the door handle, smiling, though she sensed a sudden strain. 'Thank you, but no. Why not ask Kirsty?'

He blinked and sat very still. Then he said, 'Kirsty isn't in my employ.' There was a dangerous quietness in his deep voice.

It occurred to her that this was probably the first time she'd not fallen in with anything he suggested. Ten years ago she'd been the junior partner. So madly, joyously in love. So eager to please.

He got up and strolled towards her, his hands shoved in his pockets. 'What makes you think you have a choice?' He spoke casually enough, but there was an autocratic note in the words that disconcerted her.

'Well… You must see it's not a good idea.'

'In what way isn't it?' His blue eyes narrowed, making an infinitesimal flick to her mouth even in his displeasure. Though cool, relaxed, there was alertness in his stance. 'This is a perfect solution to a glitch in the system. Do you have some commitment that prevents you from travelling?'

She shrugged. 'Not really.'

'Then what's the trouble? Is there something you're afraid of?'

Her heart thumped into its adrenaline rhythm. 'You could say so.' As he tilted his handsome head interrogatively she said, 'We're finished, Joe. Remember? That book is closed.' Adding softly, 'The song has ended, lover.'

For seconds he looked thunderstruck. Then he gave a small, incredulous laugh. 'You're leaping to conclusions, Mirandi. You've misunderstood what I…' A flush darkened his lean cheeks. 'That brief *song* was a lifetime ago, darling. You need to get over it.'

Her anger surged. 'As I recall it lasted a whole year. I wouldn't have called it brief. And I am over it. Well and truly, Joe, though I wonder if you can say the same.' Her treacherous voice wobbled.

He looked amused, though his eyes blazed bright in a way she recognised as signalling he was angry. It was such a rare look with him, the few times she'd seen it she'd been shaken, since there had to have been some major cause to disturb his usual lazy good humour.

But he controlled it, challenging her assertion with an infuriating crispness. 'On what grounds do you say that? Because I asked you on this trip? The trip is about business, pure and simple. It's an assistant I'm in need of here, not a—a—sleeping partner.'

'All right. If you say so.' She lifted her shoulders. 'I'm sorry. Though I'm not an assistant, am I?' she couldn't resist pointing out. 'I'm a market analyst, though people could be forgiven for not knowing that. Even poor Ryan seems to think I'm there as his assistant.'

Blue sparks flared in his eyes. 'You were never there as his *assistant*, but I'm glad you brought up the subject of Patterson.' His accusatory gaze lasered through her skull. 'Before you fling yourself into his bed you should know the firm doesn't encourage liaisons between personnel.'

She laughed in his face. '*What?* Oh, that's… That's just ridiculous.' Then she stared at him in shocked disbelief as the import of his words sank in. Had she heard aright? 'I don't know what you're even talking about. As if I *would*…'

He rode roughshod over her denial, striding about with an imperious air and flinging his hands about to defend himself.

'My choosing *you* is purely a business decision. As CEO I seek ways of wringing the best from my staff. You seem so— *volatile* whenever we meet…'

'*I* seem volatile?'

He ignored her interruption. 'Taking you on this trip seems like a way to develop a—a working relationship with you. Investment banking can be a soulless world. People feel out of place in it. I was hoping to establish some trust with you, to help you feel—'

She made a smouldering grimace. 'Oh, trust. Have you ever known what that was?'

He spun around to impale her with a glare. She felt the blue flash sear straight through her and knew she'd struck home. Truth to tell, she was feeling a little volatile right then, what with Kirsty and the shot about Ryan and all. Her heart was pounding like a mad thing, and she was trembling, no longer in total control of her tongue.

'On what grounds should I trust you, Joe? I was hired as a market analyst, and I've been sidelined into fetching and carrying for Ryan Patterson for the last month. I'm sure that was a perfect system solution for you, but it's not what I was promised. It's an outrageous breach of—the *law*.'

An angry flush darkened his harsh cheekbones. 'It's perfectly within the law, Mirandi. The—the arrangement was purely for your own benefit. While you work for me you fulfil any role I assign to you.'

A red-hot wave sizzled her face then rushed straight up through the top of her scalp. 'Oh, no, I don't,' she snapped. 'Because, as of this moment, I *quit*.'

He stilled and stared at her, his narrowed eyes glittering. 'You can't be serious. For what good reason?'

'For the good reason that I don't want to work for a man who doesn't keep his word.' Her voice shook with emotion. 'You haven't changed, have you? I don't know why you're so bothered about me refusing to go with you. I bet you've got stacks of reserves you could draw on.'

He froze and his eyes iced over, as chill as an arctic wasteland. After a nerve-racking second he said in a dangerous voice, 'Are you sure it's me you don't trust, sweetheart, or yourself? How long is it since I found you lolling on my bed? A whole thirty minutes?'

She couldn't trust herself to reply coolly, that much was certain. But she did manage to retort in a gravelly voice, 'I'm not your sweetheart, Joe. And that's the point.' Then she walked out and flung the door shut.

CHAPTER FOUR

JOE was running along the familiar pavement, past the garden house with the roses, around the corner house with the stone lions, and into the leafy street winding up to his place, his cricket bag knocking against his hip with every stride.

Someone would be there waiting for him. Home again at last to fill the house with flowers, laughter and her own sweet fragrance. Dinner in the oven. He felt a sudden cold fear that he wouldn't be in time. If he didn't hurry faster she wouldn't be able to wait and she'd be gone. He tried to run faster, but the way was uphill, his bag heavy and his legs wouldn't work properly.

He tried and tried to make them work, until his breath was coming in painful gasps, his lungs ready to burst, his cricket bag a leaden weight on the steep slope. With all his might he fought to gain traction on the cement path, but it was futile, the ascent changing to slippery glass and almost vertical, then just when he thought he must slide backwards he saw the yellow taxi.

It came down the hill fast, the passenger in the rear. It slowed as it approached him, and this time he could see the passenger's face. With a sickening shock he saw it was his mother. He waved at her, then as it drew level he ran shouting into the street, frantic to attract her attention, but though she looked right at him he mustn't have recognised him, because she turned her face away.

He woke with a start and lay there in the dark, bathed in sweat, waiting for the pounding brick in his chest to slow its wild *ker-thunk*. After a while he reached for the light, and the familiar solidity of his room swam into reassuring focus.

He rubbed his eyes. For God's sake, he hadn't dreamed of the yellow taxi in years. After a few minutes of slow, calm breathing he got up and thudded to the kitchen, filled a glass with water, and drank long and deep.

Something had stirred up the old nightmares, and it hardly took Sigmund Freud to work out what it was. *Who.*

In some bizarre way, Mirandi seemed to have become tangled up with his subconscious dramas. The afternoon's scene swam back to him with its astounding conclusion. Probably because of his tension about the trip, he'd felt quite churned up for a minute or two there. Completely out of character for him these days.

Mirandi was like a clover bindi underfoot. Soft, lush and enticing on the surface, with an ability to prick a man where it stung, work her way under his skin and give him everlasting grief.

Something about her had always made him feel twitchy and energised, even after a fight, though this one had ended entirely the wrong way and left him hanging off a cliff.

He set down his glass and sank onto the bed. Why did she have to be so prickly? She'd never been like that before; he remembered her as always being so soft and giving. Hell, today she'd been downright forceful.

For God's sake, the past was gone with all its wounds and it was time to move on. There was hardly a thing a man could say to her that didn't arouse some sort of touchy rejoinder. It wasn't as if he'd been unpleasant to her. Most of his employees would have jumped at the chance to accompany him to Monaco.

He felt a burning sense of injustice. A boss had every right to expect compliance from his employees. He'd only wanted to be generous with her. Why had she taken such a suspicious view of his perfectly appropriate proposition? How dared she challenge his authority. Dammit, who was running the show, he or Mirandi Summers?

He sprang to his feet again and paced the room.

It was clear she was still hooked on the dynamics of the old relationship. He should have made her understand somehow that now he was her boss the old formula could no longer work.

But for a few minutes there today… Guilt crept through him and he was swept with remorse. Now she was out of a job. Wasn't he responsible in some part at least for failing to help her make the transition? He really should have taken more care with her. Talked with her more, shown her how things stood between them now. The Patterson strategy hadn't helped either. She seemed to feel so confident she could hold her own, perhaps he should have just thrown her into the deep-end and let her sink or swim.

The image rose before him of her shapely form lying indolently on that very bed like some dreamy Lorelei. He'd rarely been so ravished. That intriguing glimpse of her private self had delivered the sweetest shock he'd known in years. He couldn't remember feeling so affected. Not since…the old days.

Had her breasts always been so full? Memories of an afternoon in Lavender Bay with her lissom body astride him, her naked breasts, their sweet taut raspberries in tantalising proximity to his mouth, made a sudden alluring appearance in his mind and he felt his blood quicken with sweet, heavy heat.

Strangely, today things had spun out of control. How much had been his fault? All he'd wanted was a little conversation, some civilised attempt at smoothing the way between them for the sake of future intercourse.

He closed his eyes. *Oh, Joe, Joe.* Where had that sprung from? Of all the Freudian slips.

Call it regret or natural concern, but he couldn't bring himself to believe he'd allowed her to walk out so abruptly. Was he to just let her go and make no effort to fix things? Surely masculine honour demanded that when he strolled onto that plane tomorrow, Mirandi Summers should be right there beside him.

Filled with sudden purpose, he strode into his study and picked up his diary to riffle through to the page of last month's board meeting. Here it was, the place where he'd absent-mindedly doodled her address.

3/ 357 Lilac Crescent, Lavender Bay.

At sight of the address a dark claw pinched his gut. The pretty little corner of Sydney he'd sworn never to set foot in again in his life. Nightmare territory.

Mirandi tossed on her bed, trying to find a comfortable position. Had her pillow always been so flat and hard? She tried to punch it into some sort of supportive mound.

Her angry tears had left a damp patch right in the spot where she wanted to rest her cheek. She hadn't felt so awful in years. Her chest hurt as if she'd swallowed something nasty that had failed to sink beyond a certain point. And the worst part was, she knew she deserved it. She'd sunk her own boat.

What sort of fool was she to have taken the job at MPI, anyway? Joe didn't want her there. He'd never wanted to see her again in his life. He'd made that plain ten years ago.

As for letting herself be caught on his *bed*…

She couldn't restrain a moan. How could she have? Was she *insane*?

Hot waves of anguish swept through her every time she thought of the moment he'd appeared in his bedroom doorway, and she couldn't hold back the tears of mortification. To be found like that after he'd *rejected* her. Even a village idiot would have had more control. More self-respect.

No one would be so stupid as to let themselves be caught in that situation after that devastating rejection. No one.

As for walking like a goddess… It was all very well to stride out of his apartment triumphant, crowing to herself over having shown him, but she'd done herself out of a job, after boasting to all her friends about having won it. Her father and Mim had been so proud. Her first proper opportunity to be a straight market analyst. Now what would she tell them?

Why had she let her emotions take over? It was just as Joe had said. She was too emotional for an MA job, any kind of job. She should be locked up somewhere remote with water access only. She'd allowed herself to get all stirred up over that Kirsty as if Joe had still been hers, when…face it. She didn't know a thing about what had gone on between them.

The truth was, admit it, she just couldn't stand to hear of him being in a relationship with *anyone*. No wonder he'd made that humiliating crack at the end. He probably thought—no, he definitely thought—the old fires were still there underneath, blazing away.

She'd exposed so much of herself she could die.

Visions of how sexy he'd looked at the end, all stern and hard and angry while he taunted her about lolling on his bed, came back to haunt her, and against all her pride and principles she couldn't suppress a sick pang of yearning.

For heaven's sake, her evil genius whispered, she could have been on a plane to France with him tomorrow if only it hadn't been for her stupid pride and her wicked temper.

After a long miserable while she realised that she'd have to start job-hunting the next day, and if she didn't act fast she'd have red swollen eyes.

She got up and tiptoed out to the kitchen in an effort not to wake her flatmates, opened the fridge and dug around in the vegetable crisper for a cucumber. Failing to find one, she settled for a courgette. Surely they had antioxidants?

She cut a few slices without much hope, then lay back on her bed and spread them over her face and eyes. Redheads were blotchy enough to start with, and it would take more than a courgette to fix her issues. She couldn't imagine what Joe had ever seen in her in the first place.

Joe's dashboard digital showed 1:58 a.m. He sighed. With a twenty-six-hour flight ahead of him, wouldn't it have been sensible to sleep? Though what was sleep? He hadn't had eight straight hours for weeks, ever since the casino project... *No.* Since Mirandi Summers had sashayed back into his life.

He turned into Lilac Crescent and slowed in an attempt to make out the house numbers. Moonlight washed the sleeping avenue in shadows, making it ideal territory for ghosts, though thankfully no ravaged, broken face of Jake Sinclair lurched out of the dark to greet him. The contours of the street had changed a little, but it was still all nerve-rackingly familiar. He felt suddenly aware of his blood pressure.

In chinks between apartment buildings he could see the city scrapers, the lights from an occasional vessel on the harbour. He supposed it was a desirable address for the innocent. Why did Mirandi still have to cling here, though? Was her father still appointed to the church here?

Indigo Street and the Sinclair house was just over the hill and around the corner, but Joe wasn't tempted. He shut it out of his mind.

The illuminated number on a high brick fence caught his eye. So this was where she'd made her home.

He drew up at the kerb. The enormity of what he was about to do, waking her and probably her flatmates in the dead of night, struck him, and he hesitated, but only for an instant. His father had always said it did no good when negotiating with a woman to start on the back foot. Not that poor Jake had wrung much benefit from his own advice.

The low buzz of the security intercom startled Mirandi from the doze she'd finally drifted into. One of the other tenants, she thought hazily, forgotten their key and mistaking the number. She settled back for sleep.

The buzzer sounded again, this time in a series of imperious staccato bursts.

Oh, for goodness' sake. Did they want to wake the whole street? Groggily, she dragged herself up and staggered out to where the intercom was fixed in the kitchen.

'Who is it?' she snarled when she'd located the button in the dark. 'Are you trying to wake the dead?'

'It's Joe.'

Shock followed fast by adrenaline sent her heart ricocheting around her chest cavity. 'Joe.'

'Yeah. Look, I, er— Sorry, I know it's late but I need to talk to you.'

Her brain made a wobbly spin. *'Now?'*

'That's right. Can I come up?'

She shut her eyes and made an attempt to think. What possible reason could he have unless it was to talk her out of quitting? An energising hope sprang up in her heart. Maybe… maybe she was still in with a chance?

'Mirandi?'

'Oh, well…' She remembered her bare blotchy face. No one should ever see her like this, let alone Joe, and in this extreme situation. 'No,' she breathed. 'Give me a minute and I'll come down.'

It might have taken more than a minute to smooth on a thin layer of make-up, perhaps two, three or even five minutes to achieve the natural look she aspired to, though she hurried as fast as she could for fear of him changing his mind and driving away. Finally she wrapped herself in her robe and flew downstairs to the entrance.

She paused to steady herself, then took a deep breath and opened the heavy door a crack.

Joe was standing on the porch surveying the street, his brows drawn. He was in jeans and a black tee shirt that stretched over his powerful chest and shoulders. His bronzed arms looked so satisfyingly solid that despite everything she felt her heart pound. Even in extremis she wasn't immune to their seduction.

He turned sharply, and she noticed his dark beard devastatingly in evidence. Hot gleams made his eyes burn when he saw her in her robe and slippers. His thorough, all-encompassing survey made her feel intensely female and vulnerable.

Remembering the way his eyes darkened like that under certain stimuli, she drew the robe closer about her. 'This—this is a surprise.'

'Yeah. Well…' He frowned, though that gleam still shone in the darkened depths. 'I've been thinking about this afternoon. I thought—maybe you'd like to talk.'

Hope fluttered in her heart but she barely allowed herself to breathe. 'About what?'

'Your decision. Were you planning to quit before today?' His hot gaze held hers for a dizzying second, then drifted down to her throat and the opening of her robe.

She dropped her lashes and shrugged. 'Well, no. Probably not. I was… I had hopes that…somehow the job might eventually work out.' She drew her fingers through her hair and his sharp glance followed the gesture, fastening on her loose tumbled locks with wolfish intensity.

His voice deepened. 'I'm pleased to hear you say that.' He scrutinised her for a moment, then the shadow of a smile touched his sensuous mouth. 'I think…er…today maybe things got a bit overheated. Things were said that shouldn't have been.'

She gave a stiff nod of admission, and as she moved further into the light his gaze sharpened on her face and she wondered if her make-up was letting her down. She edged back, but a frown entered his dark blue eyes.

'Were you asleep?'

'Of course.'

'Alone?'

She gasped. 'Yes. *Alone*. Though why you should think you can ask—'

He gestured. 'Sorry. I'm sorry, honestly. I don't know why I said that.'

A hot retort rose to her tongue, but she managed to repress it. Despite her natural annoyance at such masculine impertinence, her brain cells perked up. Why would he ask such a question if he wasn't at all interested in her? Why would he even *be* here? Surely…surely this was how the old Joe Sinclair had always operated at the time when he was crazy about her.

He resumed his smooth CEO expression, but she could feel his scorching gaze on her mouth and breasts and sense the hot magnetic current emanating from him. It sparked her nerves and made her feel extremely conscious of her nakedness under her flimsy night things.

He continued, devouring her with his eyes. 'I probably asked because I was needing to ascertain how available you are for—this offer.'

She elevated her brows. 'What offer?'

He didn't smile, but there was a burning intensity in his gaze that seared straight through her robe, her nightie and into her rapidly churning bloodstream. 'I thought you might like your job back. Interested?'

Interested. Such a flood of relief coursed through her she wanted to burst into rapturous smiles, but she knew better than to appear too pathetically grateful. 'Are we talking about my *real* job, Joe, or the job as Ryan's assistant?'

He lowered his eyelids briefly. 'Look, you were never Ryan's *assistant*. But—all right…' He lifted his hands. 'I admit we should have moved faster in setting up your office. That situation will be rectified at once if you still want the job. Okay?'

She nodded, though a joyful pulse started pumping through her veins and she wanted to sing, dance, frolic in the moonlight, maybe even throw her arms around him.

Instead she controlled herself and said with hauteur, 'Since you ask, I dare say I could—reconsider. I haven't taken on anything else yet, so…'

'Good.' His lashes flickered down but not before she saw his gleam of satisfaction. Almost imperceptibly he moved closer to her. His chest wasn't too far from her breasts. She could feel the heat from his big lean body sear her, teasing her erotic zones into an electric arousal she had no right to be feeling.

Short of breath, she edged back out of range. Heavens, how could she be so affected? So he smelled good and looked hot. Just because they were alone out here in the dark did she have to be at the mercy of her senses?

He inclined his head towards her. 'Where's that rose fragrance coming from? Is it perfume?'

She felt herself flush all over, though in a pleasant way. 'Bath oil, if you must know.'

'Oh, the old bath oil. Right.' His sensuous mouth quivered and the depths of his eyes burned brighter. 'Good. Oh, and, er—there's a condition.'

Right. With a pang of misgiving, she folded her arms under her breasts and braced for it. 'I might have known.'

Without blinking he said, 'I need you to come with me on the trip to Provence.'

An irrepressible, weakening thrill shot through her, but though the temptation to cave in was overwhelming she couldn't let go of her pride altogether. She drew herself up to stand straight and tall. 'I thought I had made it clear—'

'You did. You made it clear. But this is the condition. Take it or leave it.' His tone didn't waver while his unequivocal gaze compelled hers with mesmerising power.

She had no doubt he'd drive the bargain to the limit and walk away if she refused. Questions reeled through her head. What about the dangers? The possibilities she hardly dared even contemplate?

'Why, Joe?' she hedged. 'Why me?'

'Isn't it obvious? I need a market analyst along.'

'Oh, *right*.' She gave a disbelieving laugh, though she was excited. So excited. 'That's not what you said this afternoon. So really. Tell me what this is about.'

He hesitated. His black lashes swept down, then he pierced her with one of those glances. 'Well… I guess…it's a long trip. I'm not exactly looking forward to it and…' He exhaled in a long sigh and spread his hands. 'Somehow it would feel *right* to have you—someone I know, I mean,' he added hastily, 'along.'

Frowning, she searched his face, the involuntary leap in her heartrate warring with some warning bells that were suddenly jangling an urgent message. A message she wasn't so keen to hear. 'I don't know…'

'Do you want your job back?' A silky seductiveness had entered his voice, and he lifted one brow, assured, persuasive.

She bit her lip, hesitating, then shrugged. 'You know I do.'

'Fine. It's yours.' He smiled and warmth of a different sort, the sort of intimate, friendly warmth she used to see in the old Joe, flooded his eyes and rayed like the sun into her arteries.

For a breathless moment she almost expected him to kiss her or touch her at the very least, but he did neither. Instead he reverted to his brisk boss demeanour.

'All right, you'd better get some sleep. Check-in's at noon.' He drew his brows in admonition. 'And for once in your life don't be late.' He waited for her obedient nod, then, lifting a casual hand, turned for the porch steps.

She pulled herself together. 'Wait. Wait, Joe.'

He paused and glanced back. 'Something worrying you?'

'Yes, there is.' She braced. 'All right, I'll come, but I have a condition of my own.'

His brows went up interrogatively.

She looked steadily at him. 'You don't try to use this as an opportunity to seduce me.'

His brows flew higher still and a laugh sprang into his eyes, then he put his hand over his heart. 'Mirandi. What sort of guy do you think I am?'

'You forget,' she said without smiling. 'I know exactly what sort of guy you are.'

Her words were soft on the night air, but they must have reached their target for the lines of his face froze. Fleetingly, but perceptibly, then a muscle moved in his lean cheek and he shrugged. 'You *think* you know. But, all right, I'll accept your condition. So long as you agree to it.'

She lifted her brows. '*I* agree?'

'Of course.' Amusement tinged his lean face and his gaze sparked with challenge. '*You* must agree not to try to seduce me.'

'Oh,' she scoffed, rolling her eyes. 'As if there was ever any likelihood of that.' She gave a tinkling little laugh, then his knowing glance met hers, loaded with everything that had ever happened between them, every clinch, every wild act of passion, and she felt her face go pink.

'So, then,' he said, backing away, the gleam in his eyes. 'I'll let you know if there's any problems reserving your place on the flight. Otherwise... Noon at the International check-in. Oh, and—bring your passport.'

She damped down her mad, joyful desire to whoop down the street. 'Certainly, Joe,' she said. 'Noon.'

CHAPTER FIVE

ONLY an idiot or someone very desperate would have agreed to fly across the world with a man who'd broken her heart. And on such short notice. For a thrilled second last night on the doorstep Mirandi had actually had the sensation she was about to climb back on the Ducati.

Looking back, she suspected she might have gone a little crazy since walking into Joe's apartment yesterday afternoon. Still, a woman needed a job, and at least she'd insisted on her condition, flimsy though it might have been.

The truth was, despite her excitement, when he'd turned and walked to his car last night she'd been in a turmoil. Certainly he'd seemed appreciative of her appearance, but he'd made no move towards her—and she was grateful for that, wasn't she? After everything, especially the volcanic emotions of their afternoon encounter, it was certainly best they avoid complications and stick to their working relationship.

Still, no live woman in proximity to Joe's lips after midnight could be blamed for hungering for them. After she'd bounded upstairs to bed, all churned up and excited by the transaction on the doorstep, she was ashamed to admit she couldn't stop thinking about how sexy he'd looked with the heavy shadow outlining his mouth.

It seemed she could control her will now when it came to Joe, but there was no controlling her body. Everything about him was too deeply embedded in her senses. At least she knew now she must fight the attraction. And she could. As long as he kept his distance she'd be fine, she firmly believed it. Certainly she'd had no power of resistance when she was a green girl. But she wasn't a green girl any more.

As soon as she spotted him in Departures at noon, several things hit her between the eyes at once. He looked like an intriguing mixture of the corporate Joe and the old Joe. With his long, lean frame clad in blue jeans, loafers, and a blue shirt that reflected his eyes and brought out the highlights in his raven hair, he could have slung her over his handlebars and roared away in a second. Just as well for one of her impulsive temperament that he was carrying a casual navy jacket slung over his shoulder and his briefcase. It added that soupçon of discreet elegance the younger Joe had never aspired to.

Another thing, he was leaning against a column, brooding and looking more than a little tired. Hardly surprising, considering his habit of making nocturnal visits, though when she first observed how grim he looked she experienced a pang. Was he regretting the invitation?

He glanced up, saw her and his expression lightened at once. Her heart made a joyous little skip. That first glimpse meant truth. No chance to pretend.

She herself hadn't managed any sleep at all, she'd been so excited, wired about what to pack and doubtful. Wary. *Amazed* Joe was so keen to have her along. And in the blackest night before dawn, filled with misgivings. Warning herself not to be too thrilled. What felt so right about taking her? What had he mean by it, really?

Just take it calmly, don't be a fool, act like an MA, don't fall in love, forget the past... Oh, for goodness' sake. Under no circumstances should she allow herself to forget the past.

As Joe scrutinised her in her own jeans and jacket with a thorough, veiled gaze she enquired, 'Have you fixed the flights? Did you talk to Ryan? Should I phone him myself?'

'Relax. Everything's under control. So far,' he muttered in a grim undertone.

She shot him a quick glance. 'It's not too late to change your mind, Joe. You don't have to go through with it.'

'Of course I have to. It's my job.'

'Taking me, I mean.'

'Oh, that.' He smiled and touched her cheek. 'Oh, but I do. You're the essential ingredient.'

'Yeah?' She tried to look nonchalant, but the truth was, though it might have been a strange thing to say, those words and that careless brush of her cheek sizzled into her capillaries and radiated glowing embers through her bloodstream. It was the first time he'd actually touched her since…all those years ago.

She'd had no idea her skin was so in need of a masculine touch. So deeply in need. 'As your Market Analyst.'

'What else?'

'I hope you haven't forgotten my office.'

He spread his hands. 'In progress as we speak.'

'Good.' She beamed and he acknowledged it with a wry smile. Then his brow corrugated, almost as if he was worried.

On the flight, she threw herself into her MA role with enthusiasm.

'What's the theme of the conference?' she enquired, nestled into her business class seat sipping lemonade through a straw.

Joe frowned ahead into space, seemingly reluctant to answer.

'Making money any way we can,' he growled at last. 'What else?'

'Sounds good. Talk me through the agenda.'

He was lounging back, his eyes nearly closed, but she could see their glint through the dark lashes. His deep voice had a smoky sensuality. 'Do you still have that sexy little vest you used to wear? What was it you called it? You know...' He painted a curvy outline with his hands.

She sent him a repressive glance. 'You may be referring to a bustier. Are you sure it was me who used to wear it, or one of your chicks?'

'It was you. I'm sure it was you. I remember because it was the same bluey green as your eyes.'

She rolled her eyes. 'I doubt if *they* had much to do with it.'

He gave a lazy, reminiscent laugh. 'Oh, I can assure you, baby, they had everything to do with it.'

As the hours flew by he grew increasingly flirty and difficult to pin down about work. She'd brought her laptop, and expected to spend at least part of the flight going through the agenda with him. He should at least brief her about the appointments he'd set up with other delegates. Every time she suggested it he changed the subject.

All right, so he didn't feel like concentrating. She wished he'd tell her more about what to expect, though. How was she to do the job operating in the dark, so to speak?

He'd always been the same, as she recalled. Loath to open up. He was such a private guy, the year they'd been lovers he'd hardly even told her a thing about his family, except a few rare, affectionate allusions he made to his father. Though Jake Sinclair had died a bitter, broken man according to Auntie Mim, who'd even hinted that he'd chosen to abandon his teenage son and die by his own hand, Joe had never seemed to harbour any resentment towards him.

At least, ten hours into the flight he was looking slightly less gloomy. Devastating, in truth, lounging back in his seat, his blue shirt rolled back a little at the cuffs to reveal his sinewy forearms. It was probably safer for her not to look at him, though when she looked elsewhere his image stayed etched on her retina like a solar flare.

His book lay open on his lap but he wasn't reading. She

leaned over and flipped it to the cover. *High Finance and Ethics.* Whew. The guy really liked to relax on a flight.

'Will there be anyone you know at the conference?'

'I sincerely hope not,' he growled.

She lifted her brows in surprise. 'No, really? No old banking friends from the past?'

He looked amused. 'Bankers don't make friends, they just make money.'

She laughed, wincing. 'That's such a bleak outlook. How lonely you make it sound.'

'Well, isn't it?' He smiled, watching her face with curiosity. 'You'll find it out soon enough if you stay in it.' He gave his head a small shake. 'A crusader like *you* in investment. I have to say I was surprised.'

She gazed wonderingly at him. 'It doesn't have to be the way you describe, though, does it? Good things can be done with money. It just takes enough good people to influence an organisation to make a real difference in the world.'

Joe saw the shining conviction in her eyes and felt a pang in his chest. Even now that passion was still bubbling through her like a constant spring. Her enthusiasm for righting the world's wrongs had struck such a resonant chord with him back then. How enchanted he'd been. He realised there'd been no one in his life since with quite that quality.

'I hope you find you can hold onto your ideals,' he said quietly.

She turned an unnervingly perceptive glance on him. 'Is it that hard, Joe?'

Only a constant clench in the gut. But he had to admit it was a relief to talk about it, even so lightly. And he was impressed at her quick understanding. He examined her, trying to reconcile the woman she'd become with the girl he'd known. Maybe this was what he'd been missing. A woman he could talk to.

He yawned and stretched his long frame, then leaned across

and patted her knee. 'Don't worry, I'm sure you'll still find a way to save the world.' He tightened his hand on her knee, savouring its sensual shape against his palm.

Mirandi waited a second, then coolly removed his hand and placed it firmly on his side of the barrier.

He laughed, while her knee felt deprived.

Still, she was pleased to hear him laugh. Since the airport there'd been a tiny, permanent crease between his brows, and now she zeroed in on the grim little lines around his mouth. She guessed it wasn't all champagne and roses being the CEO.

He noticed her gaze and gave his jaw a rub. 'What? My beard still fascinate you?'

She gave his advancing shadow a wry inspection. The black fuzz hadn't even made it to the stubble stage, though it had the tantalising effect of outlining his chiselled mouth and making his lips seem sexier than ever.

'You're overstating, as usual,' she said. 'It has a long way to go before it can rate as a beard. As for whether it *still* fascinates me, that implies it ever did.'

A sensual gleam warmed his eyes and his expressive mouth edged up a little at the corners. 'Admit it.' His deep voice was low and silky. 'It's the best you've ever rubbed up against.'

She lowered her lashes, sipped her lemon squash, took a moment to contemplate an elderly woman's progress down the aisle. Then she turned to meet his sleepy, teasing glance.

'The brashest, maybe. The cockiest. Certainly the most conceited.'

His deep laugh broke out and illuminated his face. 'You've become very sassy along the way, Miss Summers. Don't you know that can get you into trouble?'

His sensuous mouth held the smile for a few extra heartbeats and there was seduction in his eyes.

Mirandi felt her heart lurch with the old dangerous thrill. But it was only banter, wasn't it? A few harmless flirty words were only natural between a man and a woman confined together in a travel situation. It didn't signal anything, or promise that anything might happen between them later.

So, regardless of how sexy he looked, how desirable he was making her feel, she was still on the straight and her conscience was clear. Strangely though, Marilyn Monroe seemed to take over her voice and she became quite breathy, as if his grin had soaked into her bloodstream and taken up the oxygen.

She made an effort to keep her mind on the matters at hand. 'Don't you just love a conference?'

'No.'

'Why not? You get to travel, have a free holiday, meet people…'

He scowled. 'There are people in Sydney.'

'Well,' she said, exasperated, 'if it's such a bore why didn't you send someone else along?'

'Because I have to go myself.' He gestured with some impatience. 'I'm researching a project the board is keen to invest in.'

'What project?'

He hesitated, then with a careful lack of expression, said, 'Investing in the entertainment industry.'

'Really? How exciting. There's big dollars to be made there.'

He searched her face, a frown in his eyes, then gave a shrug. After a while he leaned across and tucked a lock of hair behind her ear.

First her knee, now her hair. And there had been the cheek, though maybe that didn't count. Her ear tingled, and she met his hot, slumberous gaze with the blandest one she could manage, considering her blood was quickening its flow, seething with the old anticipation. She knew what those touches signalled.

Temptation was lurking in the grass and she was faced with a dilemma. A crossroads was approaching.

While she mused on the fraught possibilities, she continued on with the easy chat. 'Why don't you look on the trip as a lovely break? The south of France, of all places. Who wouldn't want to go there?'

He must have suddenly felt tired because he tilted his chair back and closed his eyes. She could tell he was still listening though by the tense way his arms were folded across his belt.

'It must be one of the most charming locations in the world.'

'Charming.'

'But you don't care for it?' After a while he shrugged, and she said, 'How many times have you been there?'

He was silent for an age. She started to repeat her enquiry when he growled, 'Once.'

'For how long?'

He frowned and opened his eyes. 'A weekend. What is this? The inquisition?'

'Must have been a lousy weekend.'

His patience snapped. 'Aren't you tired?'

She settled back into her seat. 'I remember that about you now. You always get grumpy when you're in need of sleep.'

His eyes sparked. 'And I remember things about *you*. One of them is that you're too nosy by half.'

Smiling, she tilted her seat into horizontal position, arranged the pillow, pulled the blanket over her and closed her eyes. Some bell rang in her memory, some distant echo from an old conversation, but when she tried to pin it down it slipped away. But give it time. It would come back.

She let herself drift into a doze.

When the blessed silence had settled for a while, Joe opened his eyes. Sleep was too risky here in a public space. Last thing he wanted was to be bellowing out about yellow taxis in front of several hundred people. He pulled his chair upright and took the opportunity to examine Mirandi Summers' unguarded face.

Something about the honest freshness of it put that twinge back in his chest again. Hell, he'd been through a dozen women since—maybe even a couple of dozen if he was to be honest with himself—but no break-up had been as rugged as that one. Possibly because the fling hadn't run its full course when it hit the wall at top speed. He hadn't had time to get bored, and she'd stayed fresh in his memory. Unspoiled.

He smiled to himself. That effervescent optimism was so infectious.

If this had been his first trip to Provence, he might even have shared it. He felt that wall of distaste again, and crushed it down. Since he *had* to be there, he'd focus his mind squarely on his task, think about the firm's bottom line, and get out as soon as he decently could. This hangover from his recent rash of nightmares would soon dissipate.

It wasn't as if any unwelcome faces would be looming up out of the distant past to confront him. No one he had any remote connection with even knew he was coming, and that was how he wanted it.

It would all be cool. He'd stay well away from Antibes, keep to his end of the coast, and allow the ghosts to moulder undisturbed at theirs.

In the meantime he had the perfect antidote.

Business class meant passable meals and some quite drinkable wine, though his newest MA kept to softer drinks. Without him around to lead her astray, her father's early training had prevailed. No smoking, no drinking, no gambling. No sex with bad men?

'Red wine is good for the heart,' he urged her when the stewardess came by.

'It didn't help mine,' she said, smiling her refusal to the woman.

'What was that pledge you took when you were a little girl?'

She searched his face as if sensing a trap. Seeing her wariness gave him a slight pang of remorse. Perhaps he had been guilty of teasing her in the past for the things her old dad had taught her. Maybe he'd been a bit embarrassed, knowing how often the good honest captain had been the one to drag Jake Sinclair out of the club and bring him home to his hungry kid.

With some reluctance she admitted, 'To do the most good to the most people in the most need.'

He laughed, though the words cut him in a way he didn't care to acknowledge right then. 'I'm so glad you joined MPI.'

During the dark hours, when most people were asleep under their blankets, Joe kept himself awake by reading in the cone of light from overhead. He must have disturbed Mirandi, because she woke and squinted at him.

'Can't you sleep?'

'Shh.'

After a while she pressed the upright button on her seat. 'All right, I give up. I'm too excited now. My mind keeps spinning.'

He put his book aside and suggested they stroll up to the lounge cabin so they could talk without disturbing people. She stood up and stretched, and he caught a glimpse of her breasts outlined against the material of her shirt. It was a pleasure and a torment to walk behind her and watch the supple muscles work, the pull of her jeans, snug against her taut little arse.

Mirandi felt his eyes on her in a turmoil of feelings she didn't care to acknowledge. She could sense his desire and she was affected, there was no denying it. The attraction was still there. Just a few hours in his company and she was savouring every move he made, every nuance. She shouldn't encourage it. She really shouldn't.

But, oh, some yearning part of her cried, it had been so long since she'd been appreciated by a truly sexy man. Shouldn't she just accept the gifts that life offered and bask in this pleasant time out of time?

There were a couple of other non-sleepers enjoying the open space of the lounge cabin. She stood a while, wriggling her toes, inviting her blood to flow to her ankles, conscious of Joe an arm's length away, leaning idly back against the bar. Too conscious. Too aware of the invisible pull. Here, a mile high, time had no meaning, as if the usual rules should be suspended.

Joe moved closer to her to make room for a newcomer at the bar. What was it about green eyes that gave a woman that look of potential mischief? He remembered the sensation he always used to have with her. Whatever they talked about on the surface, he felt that other, mysterious female complications were whirring away in her head.

He leaned her way and caught a trace of her fragrance. 'Do you still sing in the choir?'

'Not for years.' Her passionate mouth curved. 'Do you still sing in the shower?'

'Never seem to now. Funny, that.' The reminder evoked some intimate occasions where she'd been a star participant. 'You were pretty good in the shower yourself. I seem to remember you striking some high notes.'

Her shadowy emerald eyes flickered, then she turned away with a brief laugh. A low, throaty, *sexy* laugh.

'Does your father know where you are?'

She hesitated just a beat, then gave a perfectly serene shrug. 'There wasn't time to tell him, but if I had he wouldn't have been concerned.'

That little hesitation made him wonder how much the old man knew. Had she even told her father she was working for *him* now?

He searched her face. 'Wouldn't he? Even if he knew you were with that wicked Joe Sinclair?'

'Course not. He knows I'm a big girl. Anyway, he's never thought you were wicked.'

'Not even after I stormed the citadel and snatched away his princess?'

Her lips were enticing, curved in a smile. So plump and juicy and edible. 'It wasn't Dad who was so worried. It was poor Auntie Mim.'

Ah, so she still didn't know. Probably just as well, though some insane reckless impulse tempted him to push the boundaries of the subject. Maybe he should tell her, let her know her father's part in their little drama.

'Poor Auntie Mim,' he echoed, remembering the anxious little lady who could be so surprisingly fierce. 'What was she so worried about?'

Something disturbed the tranquil irises. Too late he felt the warning pang slice through him. His heart-rate bumped up a notch.

But her smile didn't waver. 'She was afraid you'd break my heart.'

For a second he wondered if the airbus engines had died and they were about to fall out of the sky. Then he realised it was his lungs that had stopped working.

Knowing she'd struck some momentous note, Mirandi parted her lips to say something to ease the thundering tension, but with a shock of primitive recognition saw his eyes darken.

He inclined his head and kissed her just as the plane gave a shudder, or it might have been herself being rocked to the foundations. His scorching lips touched hers with a blaze of delicious fire. Electricity sizzled through her like a lightning bolt and held her paralysed, while her blood lifted off in a wild erotic surge and swelled her breasts.

She was vaguely aware of a warning ping, a voice issuing

instructions over the tannoy, then the plane vibrated again and they rocked apart.

Hypnotised, she stared at him, her heart thundering in her ears, her breath coming in quick, erratic bursts. The hostess's voice sounded again, urging everyone to return to their seats and fasten their belts until they were through the bout of turbulence, but that brief searing touch of Joe's lips had aroused a flame.

The bar attendant stood by while people filed from the small cabin. Mirandi braced against the vibrations of the plane, under a spell, mesmerised by the fire in Joe's blue eyes, the tingling ache in her parched lips. The attendant watched them all leave, then headed for his own seat. As she and Joe started down their aisle Joe's hand snaked out and grabbed her wrist, and he pulled her back and bundled her into the washroom.

She should have resisted, but her blood was aroused and her brain had gone into a retreat. When had she and Joe *not* snatched every illicit opportunity? Squeezed into the impossibly narrow space, her guilty senses thrilling with forbidden excitement, she felt his strong arms around her, his chest in friction with her breasts, and forgot her resolutions. Distantly she heard the steward's warning voice, but it came from another realm.

In panting accord, their hungry lips met in a cosmic sensual collision. As Joe took hungry possession of her mouth Mirandi was oblivious to the discomfort of hard edges sticking into her, and concentrated on the familiar angles and planes of her hard, lean lover. Electricity was shooting through her flesh from every point of contact, knees, thighs, his angular pelvis, his strong chest pressing her breasts.

He tasted so good, his stern, sensuous mouth demanding her surrender with the same old sexy ruthlessness. Flickers of fire danced along her lips, fanning her hunger to a flame, and her nipples roused to hot aching peaks.

He deepened the kiss and his tongue slid inside her mouth.

Oh, it had been so long. Like a homecoming, the raw animal flavours of the man she'd loved so passionately invaded her senses with a heady rush and made her drunk. Her primal female instincts opened to sheer pleasure, craving to possess every fibre of him.

Hypnotised, in thrall to the irresistible sexual narcotic, she entwined herself around him, desire flaming in her blood like an incendiary. In enthusiastic response he dragged her even closer against his iron-hard frame. Oblivious of where she was, she let her hands rove his powerful shoulders and chest, rediscovering his lean, muscular solidity.

Every part of him felt so satisfying to her touch.

Hungrily she caressed the silky hair in his nape, enjoying the sensation on her fingertips. It was a sensual explosion. Drenched in desire, her breath mingling with his, her yearning nipples and the tender tissues between her thighs burned for his caress.

As if in instinctive understanding he slipped a hand under her shirt and pushed up her bra for an exploration of her breasts. His big warm hand felt so pleasant on her soft skin, so *right*, while his gentle tease of her nipples added fuel to the flames.

His erection prodded her, heightening her arousal. Her craving for his clever hands to roam in a southerly direction raged in her blood like wildfire.

They slid to her bottom, stroking her with a delicious touch. Urgent for contact where it counted, she made an attempt in the cramped space to hook her leg around his calf.

Obligingly, he pulled her pelvis hard against him and rotated his hips in a primitive rhythm she found wildly stimulating. While his hand squeezed one grateful breast, and his tongue tickled the delicate tissues inside her mouth, she felt his hard penis tantalise the yearning delta between her legs.

The friction was erotic, it held the promise of ecstasy, but with so many clothes in the way it wasn't nearly enough.

She reached for his belt buckle, but abruptly, and probably just in time, a sharp tattoo on the door roused her from her escalating sensual trance. Surfacing back to painful awareness of her uncomfortable surroundings, she broke from the kiss.

A glimpse of her face in the mirror acted on her hot fraught body like a douse of cold water. Panting, she pushed vigorously at Joe's chest and slapped at his roving hands.

'Stop this,' she hissed. 'Get out of here. Go on.'

He looked startled. 'Now?' he said hoarsely.

A glance into his dark inflamed eyes threatened to send her under again, but she insisted.

'Go on.' She squeezed away from the door to make space for it to open. With a last burning look at her, he edged past her and left.

She spent some time splashing her face and tidying up, alone and not regretting it, her thoughts on hold until she could bear to look herself in the face. When she emerged, the main cabin lights were back on, people were moving and shuffling around, and all the signals were there that a meal was about to be served.

Somehow she found her seat and settled back into it, fighting to compose herself and will away the sweet, insidious pleasure still mingling in her bloodstream with all the dissatisfied cravings the clinch had aroused.

Guilt washed through her, and a sobering streak of anxiety. How could she have been so weak, so thoughtless? When she had everything to lose, at the very first test of her resolve she'd fallen. She hadn't even made it through the flight without surrendering herself to him. She blenched to think of how quickly she'd succumbed.

All through the night she'd been castigating herself for not having properly ascertained what it was he expected from her on this trip. Was this it?

Shame and disappointment chilled her heart. How did he think of her? That she was his ever-ready pushover? That he could still seduce her, make her love him, then break her heart and walk away?

She tried to struggle out of her attack of conscience with a more positive view. If she'd engaged in a sexy interlude in the washroom with him ten years ago, she wouldn't have ejected him quite so soon. At least now she could congratulate herself for having drawn some sort of line.

It was hard to think clearly all churned up, but she needed to be brutally honest with herself. Had she really expected nothing to happen? Did she really *want* nothing to happen? She'd loved it when he came to her doorstep to negotiate because it had allowed her to cave in and still preserve her pride.

But while that strict little voice in her head was hauling her naked across the burning coals, there was no denying her old wild reckless part was still there, crazy to plunge straight in with him again. It was a dilemma, and it was wrong. *She* was wrong.

Although maybe it was right. Why else did it feel so right?

Oh, she was a weak, weak vessel, and she needed to put a definite distance between herself and Joe Sinclair.

She waited, tense as a wire, but he didn't return for some time. Probably gloating over his easy conquest, she glowered to herself. No doubt knocking back a triumphal Scotch.

When he did come, she had her headphones on and her book open before her. He slipped into his seat silently, with just a sidelong glance at her. She quickly lowered her eyes.

He took his own book from the seat pouch and started to read. It was like a taunt to her, how relaxed he seemed after breaking her condition. His employee, no less. He should have been ashamed.

After a long tense while, in which she hardly took in a

word of what she was reading, he put his book aside, reached across and lifted hers out of her hands.

'Talk to me.'

She lifted an earphone and gazed coldly at him, eyebrows raised. 'Sorry?'

'I don't think you should be regretting that kiss.'

A hot little pulse started up in her head. 'Don't you?' She narrowed her eyes. 'Perhaps what I'm regretting is that you seem to feel you still have the right to kiss me.'

His sleepy, sensual gaze drifted to her mouth. 'Well…it wasn't so much that I feel I have the *right*. Whoever knows he has the right? I think I feel as if I have—the connection.' He smiled, dropped her book in her lap and leaned back in his chair.

She found her page and stared at it for a while, churning. There was truth in what he claimed, of course, but could she just surrender like a weakling? But she must restrain herself from arguing with him. She knew of old that when he mocked her in that flirty way her resistance to his charm crumbled. In no time she found herself melting, smiling like a loon, and before she knew it flirting like some meowing siren. She should never allow herself to look into his eyes.

But by her honour as a woman, could she truly let him have the last word?

She stared into her book a while longer, then snapped it shut and reached across to snag his sleeve. 'You were wrong.'

'Sorry?'

'The connection is dead.'

His black brows shot up. 'Really? You mean you were faking it?' Despite his apparent cool, lounging there in his seat like a relaxed panther, his beard shadow very much in evidence, there was a sly smile in his eyes. It was infuriating. And so damnably attractive.

'You took me by surprise,' she accused, annoyed at herself for being so intensely aware of how sexy he looked. How kissable, how mouth-watering his lips were, outlined by the shadow. She could have climbed up on his lap there and then and…

The truth was, he was *driving* her to lie.

'I'm a civilised person. Naturally I didn't want to make a scene. I may have pretended to co-operate but I was only being polite.'

He smiled. '*Very* polite.'

Despite her guilty knowledge of her own disgraceful compliance, her feminine spirit rose up on its hind legs, and with it the certainty she could trust herself to be a virtuous woman from now on.

'Mock if you like,' she said crushingly, 'but you can be sure neither that kiss nor anything like it will ever happen again. Let me remind you of my condition.'

He was silent a moment, studying her face, his expression grave apart from a curious little gleam in his eyes. Then he said, 'And let me remind you of *my* condition.'

She narrowed her eyes. 'You're not trying to claim *I* started that clinch, are you?'

'Well, you were extremely tempting.' His voice had a deep, sonorous, velvety texture that crept into her bones and made them weak. 'Too tempting to resist, all soft and curvy and luscious.'

She couldn't hold back a hearty laugh, though it came out sounding a little on the silvery side. Not that she wanted to give the impression she was flattered. She wasn't a bit.

'Oh, that's nonsense,' she scoffed. 'That's as ridiculous as if I said I kissed you because you were—' she cast about for some suitable words '—*hard and sexy.*'

He gave a deep, rumbling laugh. 'Yeah. At least one of those was so, so true.' He rubbed his handsome jaw, still laughing, an amused reminiscent gleam in his eye. 'Anyway, does it really matter who succumbed to who? Once that train has left the station it hardly matters who's doing the driving, sweetheart.'

Intoxicating vibrations were weakening her, seducing her, threatening to drag her in, but she said as firmly as she could, 'Be assured, mister, the train *hasn't* left the station.'

He nodded, though that lazy smile was still in his eyes. 'If you say so. Course it hasn't.'

He relapsed into silence after that, but it was an exciting, connected silence, as if invisible wires were attached to them and primitive messages were pinging back and forth, whispering thrilling promises.

As time wore on, though, and Zurich drew closer on the radar, the transmission signals changed. Joe grew serious and more remote, as if some inner dialogue was keeping him preoccupied.

Was it about her? Was he having second thoughts about bringing her?

CHAPTER SIX

DAWN brought them to Switzerland, with a day and a night to fill before their connecting flight to Nice. As the plane circled in the lea of the Alps Mirandi caught her breath at the beauty of mist-shrouded lakes and rivers and the lushest green valleys she'd ever dreamed.

Zurich spread along the shores of a vast lake and its connecting river, a fairy tale city dotted with spires and mediaeval clock towers, magical in the crisp early morning air.

After the long flight it was a relief to check into the Chateau du Lac and relax with a warm shower and a change of clothes. Stella had arranged for an especially early check-in, and Mirandi sent the excellent woman a telepathic thank-you across the world for her efficiency and taste for the good life.

Joe had a meeting with a banker in the Bahnhofstrasse, a boulevard in the heart of the city's commercial centre, and Mirandi took some trouble in her preparations, washing her hair and straightening it dry till it hung sleek and silky down her back. It was only right she should try to look her professional best, surely. The last thing any MA/Assistant should do was to disgrace her boss in a high-level business negotiation. She wasn't trying to make herself especially gorgeous or alluring. If efficiency and grooming happened to appeal to a man... Well, then, let it be. With her conscience perfectly clear, she donned her slimmest navy suit, purple silk cami and heels, walked through a soft air-spray of perfume, then took the lift down to the hotel restaurant.

She found Joe ensconced at a window table overlooking the Zurichsee. A newspaper was spread before him, but he didn't appear to be reading. Instead he was frowning into space.

He looked so grim and preoccupied her heart lurched with anxiety. Was he thinking about her? Regretting re-opening the door to desire?

'Hope you weren't waiting long,' she said, laying her notebook in its slim leather envelope on the table.

He started from his reverie and glanced up at her. His quick smile crinkled the corners of his eyes and she felt such a relief.

'Only two newspapers' worth,' he said. 'You must have rushed.'

He looked so handsome, all freshly shaven and shower clean in his fresh suit and crisp cotton shirt, she felt a deep visceral stir in her insides so sweet and intense as to be almost like pain. She noticed him glance at her laptop, then flick an appraising blue gaze over her.

Appreciation warmed his eyes and the glow inside her intensified. Only another frizzy redhead could truly appreciate her beauty exigencies, and she was reminded that Joe could be a remarkably patient man.

'No, *you* must have dawdled,' she retorted, her pulse quickening as his sensual gaze flickered down her legs to her ankles. 'And *two* newspapers is bunkum. Your hair's still damp.'

He laughed, folded his newspaper out of the way and signalled the waiter to bring coffee and hot chocolate.

But the truth was, every little teasing exchange only increased her turmoil. It was of no use to fall in love with him again. She'd been down that road and heartache was the only destination. So, while savouring croissants with him and watching the pleasure craft on the Zurichsee might have been romantic, she couldn't allow herself to acknowledge her pleasure in his company. The more tempted she felt to surrender to her yearning instincts and plunge right in, the more her conscience and insecurities worked against her.

In twenty-four hours so many moments had revealed nuances of her old lover, still there underneath despite everything, yet she needed to remind herself that her old Joe had grown tired of her.

And she could sense a tension in him. Despite his easygoing banter, his gaze was pensive, those grim little creases around his mouth subtly deeper. He'd closed up about work, and had little to say about his plans for the day. Doubt about her professional abilities?

She frowned. She was looking forward to attending that meeting with him, learning more about MPI's operations at the highest level. After the debacle of her start with the firm, the opportunity was important to her. If she could demonstrate something of her skills and competence, Joe would see how far she'd grown beyond the raw teenager he'd once known and she could nip his reservations in the bud.

At the appointed time, she strolled along the leafy Bahnhofstrasse with him, taking pleasure in the foreign sights and smells, the trams rattling up and down the centre of the street, not exactly nervous but on her mettle to do well. The bustling city and centre of international commerce seemed remarkably clean and ordered after Sydney's grimy traffic snarls, its very pavements gleaming.

She couldn't help feeling a little smug when women they passed in the street cast sidelong glances at Joe's tall dark form. In his banker's suit, briefcase in hand, he looked as sleek and prosperous as any of the businessmen hurrying to and fro, though hotter. Far hotter.

'Here we are,' he said, halting with a light hand on her elbow.

She gazed up at the discreet façade of one of the richest banks in the world.

'Good. Now what did you say we're meeting about?'

Joe scrutinised her. The blue of her suit turned her skin to milky satin and deepened the indigo ring around her irises. In this light they were teal, their golden flecks turned amber, and he remembered with an uncomfortable twinge how clear-seeing they could be. It flashed through his mind that if she was still the girl he thought she was, her smile might not be so eager and positive when she learned what he was negotiating.

'Well, er...' He frowned and scratched his ear, evaded her gaze. 'I'm negotiating with the bank about an investment the firm is considering in Sydney. But, look, there's no real need for you to come up. Why don't you do some sight-seeing?'

Mirandi felt an acute stab of disappointment. 'But—wouldn't you like me to come with you? Take notes or something?'

He shot her a keen glance, and she read the comprehension in his eyes.

'I won't need notes.' He knew she was hurt, she could sense it, but though his eyes were rueful his tone remained cool and firm. 'Why don't you stay down here and take a look around the shops? As I recall, this street is a women's shopping paradise. I'll meet you at *that* café...' he pointed across the street at an attractive awning sheltering a mass of tables and chairs, then glanced at his watch '...an hour from now.'

She drew breath to protest, but his expression was implacable. She knew that look. There was no use arguing.

Smarting, she watched him stride away. Why hadn't he wanted her with him? He disappeared into the building and she had nothing left to do but turn and stroll along the street, an alien on the other side of the world. Exciting though it was to be set free in this charming foreign city, she was beginning to feel a bit pointless.

Go shopping, he said. Shopping! What was she, a decoration? Was he as evasive about letting Stella in on his work commitments? Visions rose in her mind's eye of Stella at work making calls, striding along beside him, greeting his clients, emerging from meetings looking secretive and important, and she decided not. No, he'd never tell Stella to *go shopping*.

She slipped her laptop into her bag and threaded her way disconsolately among the shoppers, wondering just what her role was.

There was a startling array of designer boutiques around her, some with end-of-summer sale notices posted in their windows. She stared desultorily into a couple, then conceded she might as well take the opportunity to buy something to wear for evening, since her last-minute packing frenzy hadn't allowed her time to acquire anything special.

After several boutiques she tottered out reeling from the prices. Even the most unassuming shops in this precinct were beyond her humble means. And face it. Shopping required a certain mood an excluded MA couldn't summon. With a shrug she gave up the idea of a dress and wandered along the street until a captivating glimpse of the river lured her down a side-street to the quay.

Some time later she found the Bahnhofstrasse again and hastened back to the rendezvous, scanning for Joe. Her heart skipped when she saw his tall figure, standing quietly by the café. He was leaning against the wall, arms folded across his chest, his brows lowered in brooding contemplation. Had the meeting gone badly?

She hurried up to him.

'There you are.' He straightened up, lifting his brows at her empty hands. 'What? No shopping?'

She shook her head, smiling to cover the smouldering embers of her razed self-esteem. 'Plenty of fruitless looking, though. How did your meeting go?'

For an instant his strong lean face was motionless, then he lifted his shoulders with casual unconcern. 'Probably a bit too well.'

'Oh.' She slanted him a glance. 'So they agreed with your investment in the Sydney thing?'

'Yep,' he said curtly. 'They agreed.'

'Well, that's great, isn't it?'

He shrugged. 'Of course. Great.'

But there was a shadow in his eyes and she felt confused. Of course she was being too intrusive, asking for information he clearly didn't want to discuss. Maybe there were some things an assistant couldn't be privy to, especially one who was a last-minute stand-in. Still, rationalise it as much as she might, her doubts about his attitude towards her began to intensify.

Why bring her along if he didn't trust her?

Perhaps he sensed her hurt, because he made an effort to recapture their friendly mood and suggested they stroll down to the river and see some of the sights. She agreed, grateful for a way to ease the tension. And it worked. Even the gloomiest couple in the world would have found it impossible not to smile at the swans gliding along with majestic unconcern as their anxious cygnets paddled madly to keep up. And an hour or two of wandering through the fascinating old town on the other side of the bridge smoothed over the momentary abyss in communication. Soon Joe charmed her into laughing again, teasing and flirting with her as if she were the most desirable woman in Zurich.

At lunchtime they chose a café on the busy quay, hung with pots of scarlet geraniums to match the chequered table-cloths.

'Oh, I adore Zurich,' she enthused, stretching back in her chair and glancing around her. 'I can't imagine Nice will be any the nicer.'

He smiled at her over the top of his menu, acknowledging her terrible pun. 'You'll probably love it. Millions do.'

Something stirred in her memory then and she narrowed her eyes in recollection. 'Didn't you once tell me your mother lives in Europe somewhere?'

He blinked. His lean face smoothed to become expressionless. 'Did I?'

'I'm sure you did. Didn't you say she's an artist? Does she still paint?'

His blue eyes chilled to impenetrable ice. 'I have no idea.' Frowning, he turned his attention back to his menu. 'Are you ready to order?'

She bit her lip. If that had been a rebuke she deserved it. She should have remembered how reluctant he was to talk about his mother. But after all these years, surely he must have come to terms with his dysfunctional family? Wasn't there a time to face parents as adults? Even she, a certified scarlet sinner in some people's eyes, had managed to find some common ground with her oldies. And according to Mim, who admittedly had strong opinions about everyone she knew, no woman could have put up with Jake Sinclair and the life he'd led.

They lunched on fish caught fresh from the lake, steamed green vegetables and fried potatoes served with Alpine cheese and apple sauce. Mirandi adored every delicious morsel. She battled with her conscience over dessert, but how often would she have the opportunity to taste a bona fide Swiss chocolate torte laced with cherry brandy? In the end, true to form, she gave into temptation.

Joe watched her contemplate the cake set before her with smouldering appreciation. A woman with an unashamedly healthy appetite was a woman of promise, though how she managed to maintain that tiny little waist was a mystery. She was getting to him, there was no denying. His blood quickened as he imagined unwrapping her nakedness, burying himself in her satin heat. A night with her in his arms would surely dispel that sensation he'd been waking to lately of the stone weighing in his chest. Though why wait for night? An afternoon. Hell, an afternoon *and* a night. The next afternoon, the next night…

'Want a taste?'

He watched her ripe lips close over a mouthful, and felt a dangerous stir in his loins. 'Not of the cake,' he said softly.

His burning sensual gaze seared her with unashamed lust and Mirandi felt herself lose motion, like a bird in flight about to fall from the sky, though her blood was thumping fast. The crowds, the noise of the café all receded into the distance.

Still, her heart clamoured for answers.

She lifted her gaze to his. 'I'm confused, Joe,' she said breathlessly. 'What—what am I doing here with you, really?'

He shrugged and his eyes veiled beneath his black lashes. 'I thought I explained. You're here as my—sounding board.' He opened his hands. 'Friend, if you like.'

'I don't think so.' She shook her head. 'Sounding board, MA, *friend*…' The word nearly caught in her throat with all its irony. She added quietly, 'You don't kiss friends. Not like that. I'd just like to know where you think this is going. How about letting me in on the plan?'

His brows shot up. 'There's no *plan*.' He flicked her an oblique glance, then said lightly, 'How about companion? I'm sure you can kiss a companion.'

The emotion roiling away inside her wouldn't allow her to smile. 'I'm serious. We made a condition…'

'A condition we're both guilty of breaking.'

She flushed. 'I know that. The thing is that—after the things that happened with us before, I think you should know I'm not… I have no intention of *ever*—'

He flung up a hand to stop her. 'No, *don't* say that.' His blue gaze was suddenly intent, urgent. 'Never say it. Look…' He closed his eyes an instant. 'Just—listen. How could we not kiss? As soon as I saw you again I realised… That connection with you is still so… You know, I've missed the way I used to feel with you.'

'Oh.' Her heart shook.

Perhaps she should have been more severe with him, but in

all honesty those words struck a deep emotional chord in her, rare as such admissions were from a private guy like Joe. His deep, earnest voice, his intense gaze, his beautiful gesturing hands were sincere, and, foolish or not, she believed him. So, in spite of herself, the massive barrier that had frozen there after his rejection and her bitter aftermath melted a little.

'I see,' she said, lowering her lashes while her pulse thundered in her ears. 'Well, that's really—quite—interesting to know. Only I can't—let you play on my heartstrings again, Joe.'

'Again,' he echoed sardonically, a flush darkening his cheeks. Then he added softly, 'That's a two-way street, wouldn't you say, sweetheart?'

A million retorts, questions, reproaches hovered on her tongue and the silence between them pulsed with dangerous vibrations too threatening to voice. She was the one to break it, skittering away from the seismic zone with a husky change of subject.

'So then...' scrambling into safetalk, her pulse still seething, hardly knowing what she was saying, '...at this conference, will it all be just meetings? Is there anything in particular I should be prepared for?'

He studied her with a slight frown in his eyes, then rubbed his cheek and allowed his expressive mouth to relax. A veiled gleam shot into his eyes. 'I think there's some sort of cocktail thing on one night. And maybe a dinner. Or...oh, hell. I probably should have warned you.' She started to speak but he cut in. 'No, let me make amends for—everything. If you'd like to choose something to wear while we're here, the bank will foot the bill.'

She opened her eyes wide. *'What?* Are you serious?'

'Of course.' He reached across and captured her hand. 'Don't look so shocked. I insist. I can't take my loveliest market analyst to the ball unless she's wearing the latest designer creation from Paris.'

'There's no need. I have clothes. And look. Listen, Joe…'

But despite herself, she wavered. It was an olive branch, and kindly meant. And even after her stern warning that strong warm hand clasping hers was a powerful persuader, tuning her in once again to the high-voltage electric current that until yesterday she'd been excluded from for a decade. Oh, how she'd missed it.

Fireworks were lighting her up, confusing her, muffling her self-protective instincts. She was being swept along again on that hot, wild torrent to the place where the rules of the ordinary world didn't apply, just as she had that long ago day in the churchyard.

'What are you doing, Joe?' she said weakly.

He was smiling, a caress in his voice, that desire in his kingfisher-blue eyes so affecting. It was just like the time on the plane. She shouldn't look into his eyes. She *shouldn't*.

He gave her hand a squeeze. 'I'm holding this lovely hand. I'll keep on holding it until you agree.'

Her mind raced, along with her rapid pulse. He was charming her again, undermining her resistance, seducing her. But whether she was a sounding board, MA or friend, allowing him to buy her something as intimate as a dress was against all the rules. She could see where this was headed. Straight into mistress territory.

With an embarrassed glance at the neighbouring tables she tried to tug away, though not very hard. *'Joe.'* Her voice was as croaky as a crow's. 'People are looking at us.'

'Shh. We're shocking these good Swiss. Are you ready to agree, or do we keep holding hands?' He added softly, 'I can feel your electricity shooting up my arm.'

Her heart skittered at that undeniable truth. Her skin welcomed his strong, warm clasp and never wanted to lose it. And wasn't that always the trouble? Despite the imminent dangers, she couldn't prevent her imagination from flying her to the hotel room and envisaging the likely indulgences a mistress might be expected to provide.

Joe adjusted his grip a little, palm to electric palm, watching her eyes, the smiling awareness she couldn't conceal, the desire curving her mouth, warming her neck and cheek. His instincts of imminent victory gathered certainty. For days he'd been remembering how sweet it had been with her. How giving she was. How passionate.

She gave a slightly more determined tug and he released her. Not a moment too soon, if the tightening in his underwear was anything to go by.

'Dresses are what you buy a mistress,' she reproved, but his blood surged at the capitulation in her voice.

He smiled. 'Oh, *mistress*. That's such an old-fashioned concept. It's time it was put to bed.'

'Don't use that sexy tone with me.' Her attempt at sounding stern didn't quite come off. Not with that husky breathless quality in her voice. 'Haven't I made it clear? I'm still an old-fashioned girl and I *haven't* come as your mistress. Or to be put to bed. I'm here as your sounding board, remember? Your MA.'

'And it's as my MA that I'll be escorting you to that cocktail party. And it's as your *boss* that I insist on attiring you in a manner befitting Martin Place Investments.'

'*What?*'

He was startled by the green flash in her eyes.

She leaned forward and said in a low, outraged voice, 'Are you saying—you don't feel confident in the clothes I choose? Are you afraid I'll *embarrass* you?'

Whoa there. His instincts started clanging alarm bells. Careful how you handle this one, victory guy.

'Sweetheart. No, no, sorry—*Mirandi*.' He sighed and spread his hands in rueful appeal. 'You know I think you always look *amazing*.' Words even more dangerous than before flew out before he could call them back. 'When I see you walk by at work looking so—so beautiful and luscious and clever and smart...I just...' Desire threatened to loosen his tongue beyond what was prudent, and he made an adroit sidestep. 'What I'm saying is I—I'm so glad you took the job at MPI. I know you'll be just great there. We need more people like you. And I'll be so proud of my MA at that conference.'

They must have been the right words because he saw her eyes soften and shine. He was shaken by a powerful surge of tenderness towards her, and had to fight an overwhelming impulse to say even more things. Irrevocable things.

If they hadn't been in a public restaurant he could have expressed himself properly without having to resort to words at all.

He restricted himself to saying, 'I just want to give you something—lovely. Something to thank you for coming with me. At least let's wring *some* pleasure from this bloody hell of a trip.'

CHAPTER SEVEN

NATURALLY, Mirandi caved in. Well, her knees had gone weak. Anyway, travelling with a sexy man on a short fuse when she was tired herself required a certain amount of give and take. Joe really did seem to need cheering up.

And truly, when they went strolling through the boutiques and he took her hand with the old easy familiarity, it felt so right. And it was lovely trying on beautiful things she could never have normally dreamed of. Joe was so generous and kind, like her wonderful old Joe, waiting patiently for her to make up her mind, only grinning and giving a shrug when she rejected dress after dress in shop after shop.

In fact, she kept catching him looking at her with a light in his eyes that made her blood effervesce like hot lemonade.

And he could be helpful, as she discovered when she finally tracked down the sort of dress that appealed to her in one highly exclusive couture shop. The manager was a haughty, fortyish Frenchwoman with shrewd black eyes and a tight, narrow smile.

While Mirandi sifted through the beautiful things on the racks, Joe found a wingchair thoughtfully placed outside the fitting room area and settled into it, stretching out his long legs and lounging back with a newspaper over his face.

There was much to choose from, but her final decision was between an ankle-length red satin dress with a plunging neckline and a split, and a rose-and-peach-coloured silk georgette with narrow straps and a tulip skirt. Each of them was a dream come true, though both were fearfully expensive.

She tried the georgette first. Because of its thin straps she had to remove her bra so as not to spoil the effect of the bodice. The manager hovered outside, ready to dash in at the first opportunity to snatch her sacred merchandise out of harm's way.

Mirandi allowed the woman a glimpse and *madame* was overwhelmed, at the same time as slipping in some sharp observations about how the excellence of the design concealed *mademoiselle's* imperfections. Only see how it created the illusion of breasts, and covered *mademoiselle's* too generous thighs. Such a pretty effect on *mademoiselle* with her unfortunate hair and that pallid complexion was *magnifique*, *parfait*, *incroyable*.

The sound of new customers entering the boutique cut short the stream of superlatives, and the saleswoman bustled away. Though smarting at the slurs on her beauty, it was with some regret that Mirandi carefully peeled off the gorgeous georgette, replaced it on its hanger, then turned to the red satin.

Just her luck, but once she'd poured herself into the fabulous thing and pirouetted a few times to enjoy the sensational effect of its fluid slinkiness front, rear and sideways, the zip stuck fast and she couldn't take it off.

Twisting and turning for a better angle, she struggled to shift it until she felt something give in the fabric.

Oh, *no*. She grew hot. What if she'd torn it? She'd have to call the dragon woman and confess.

She put her head out of the door, but there was a small hallway separating the fitting rooms from the sales floor and the woman was out of sight. Mirandi could hear her voice as she dealt with other customers, and her mind leaped to Joe—who she'd last seen lounging in a chair around the corner.

She poked her head out of the door and called softly to him. He appeared in the hall entrance, looking taken aback.

'I need your help,' she said in a low urgent voice. 'Can you come here a minute?'

His brows lifted, then he sauntered in and stood at the door, quizzical amusement in his eyes. 'Yeah? What seems to be the trouble?'

At the gleam in his eyes she felt misgivings along with a definite charge in her insides. 'Do you mind… Can you help me with this?' She opened the door a tiny bit wider and angled around to show him. 'See, the zip's stuck. I'm afraid I might have damaged it.'

She glanced back at him and a warm shivery sensation shimmied down her spine as his blue eyes swarmed all over her, aglow with searing, sensual admiration.

'Oh, my God, that dress.' His hands flew out, but didn't actually touch her. 'You look—like a *flame*.' His voice deepened on the word.

'All right, all right,' she said tartly, though she couldn't help but be warmed by such overt appreciation. If a woman had to be stuck inside a dress and was forced into calling a man to the rescue, it was as well the dress should be flattering.

'You do know if I've damaged it I'll have to pay for it,' she warned to dampen his enthusiasm. 'And it costs a *fortune*.'

'And worth every red cent,' he exclaimed with heartfelt warmth.

She should have known this would be a mistake. He was loving it. She looked sternly at him and he immediately put on a solemn expression.

'Do you want me to do it out here, or…?' He was trying to sound grave, but his voice had deepened to a revealing huskiness.

A dangerous intuition tingled along her nerve-endings, and her nipples reacted involuntarily, as if his bronzed hands had already brushed her bra-less breasts. This had all the hallmarks of one of those risky occasions. But her options were few.

She cast a quick glance around, then motioned him into the fitting room.

It was only a small room. Perhaps because the walls were shrinking, or because there was a forbidden quality to the situation, what with the strict Frenchwoman close by, she felt a wicked zing ripple through her bloodstream.

She faced him for a breathless second, seared to her entrails by his hot eyes and the raw animal hunger she saw there.

He must have been crazed, because he cradled her face in his hands, scorching her with his devouring gaze, and said hoarsely, 'You're still so gorgeous. You're just—gorgeous.'

Then he kissed her, a sensual tasting of each of her lips while he plundered her mouth tissues with his clever tongue. She didn't care that he was clearly short-sighted and mentally deranged. She supposed she could have interrupted and said, 'It's the *dress*, stupid,' but this wasn't the time to give him a lesson on dresses and what they could do for the female form because she was deeply into the kiss. Her bones were dissolving and she had to cling to him to support herself.

The kiss broke and he stared into her face, his eyes ablaze with two disturbing points of flame she remembered well. An age-old excitement gripped her.

For heaven's sake, some last vestige of reason clanged in her brain, they were in a boutique fitting room. She gave him a small, provocative push away, then turned her back to him and held up her hair.

The move didn't have any dampening effect, it seemed. Now his reflection smouldered before her in the mirror, lust in his eyes.

Against everything her brain knew was wise, her blood surged to the primitive call, rocking into a slow, heavy, sensual beat.

'Have I torn it?' Even to her own ears she sounded huskier than the norm.

'Just a bit.' *His* voice was deeper than a well. 'Looks like a part of the stitching's come away.'

'Shh. Keep your voice down.'

He worked at the zip, frowning in concentration, occasionally brushing her back with his knuckles. Her wanton skin welcomed every tiny contact, and each time it happened his eyes clashed with hers in the mirror and ignited more burning embers in her blood.

At last he murmured, 'There.' She felt him tug at the zip, shift it a little way, then ease it smoothly all the way down to the small of her back. Cooler air played along her spine.

'Great,' she breathed, letting her hair fall. She didn't move, and neither did he move away from her. She grew preternaturally conscious of his closeness, the tense current pulsing between them, her breasts naked under the thin red satin.

The air in the little room grew taut with risk.

His strong hands closed around her upper arms and her heart started to thud. In the mirror she saw him bend towards her. She closed her eyes, quivering as his lips scorched her nape, her flesh leaping in instant response.

He lifted his head, and she waited. She met his darkened gaze in the mirror, and saw that her own eyes were curiously dark and glowing. Her skin prickled as he ran a light finger along the ridge of her spine, igniting little streamlets of fire.

Then he paused. She dared not breathe, teetering on the verge of a tingling suspense, longing for him to touch her again. Her nipples tautened with suspense, aching, yearning to be touched.

Then, to her intense pleasure, he slid his warm hands in under the dress opening, loosening the snug bodice. He drew her against him while he held her breasts, softly squeezing and stroking them, igniting little rivulets of fire under her skin. She panted as her breasts swelled with heat, her nipples tingling as he delicately teased and taunted them with his long, lean fingers.

Fingers that were delicious enough to lick. She burned everywhere, but the wildest thirst burned between her legs, and she was seized by that old reckless sensation he'd always inspired in her and forgot all prudent considerations.

He kissed her neck and put his tongue in her ear, his hot breath tickling and inflaming the sensitive orifice.

Lucky he was supporting her with his big lean frame, because her knees nearly collapsed and she sagged against him. The mingled sensations were so pleasant and arousing, her hidden delta craved and yearned to be caressed.

Her veins seemed to flow with liquid fire as though her body were all at once bursting from its conventional constraints and longing to plunge into a wild explosion of every possible pleasure.

She tried to turn around to him to open up the possibilities but he held her severely before him. Feeling the hard length of his erection pressing into her, she reached behind her in an attempt to encourage him to hurry in their stolen hideaway. But growling something under his breath, he grabbed her hands and held them still.

His face in the mirror was so raw and naked it scorched her mesmerised gaze and she couldn't look away.

She couldn't remember feeling so hot, but still he toyed with her. He slid his hot, urgent hands caressingly over her hips and thighs as if she were some rare and precious figurine he was moulding from clay, then, when she was least expecting it, to her excitement he eased up the dress and exposed her pants and the nude pale skin at the tops of her stockings.

She saw lust flare in his eyes.

Lust was infectious. She stilled, holding her breath, her erotic tissues ignited with a desperate craving. Then fascinated, simmering with fever, she watched the reflection as his lean tanned hand slid across her navel then down beneath the elastic of the flimsy underwear.

She felt a small involuntary rush of moisture.

Panting and trembling, she could feel his hot breath on her neck. As if he understood her most intimate needs, with exquisite softness his smooth fingertips sought the delicate lips, found her sensitive, burning, engorged folds and stroked them. Found her sweetest, most delicate, most explosive spot, and caressed her there.

Ah-h-h. Rapture forced a series of little gasps from her. Then hypnotised, swooning with delight, she watched as he slid those long smooth fingers inside her.

Ecstasy.

Shuddering, her breath coming in hoarse gasps—she might have whimpered—she parted her thighs to give him more access and gave herself up to enjoyment of the forbidden magic. Just when she was climbing to a pitch of the most fantastic, blissful tension, a demanding feminine voice cut through the sultry mists of her pleasure.

'Mademoiselle. Mam'selle exige-t-il l'aide?'

She started back to reality and they both froze. 'What?' she mouthed at Joe.

He frowned and shook his head, signalling no.

'No,' she squeaked. 'No, *merci, madame*. I'm fine, and I'm coming. Now. At once.'

If only that had been true. It was the ultimate in anticlimax. Plans she'd been concocting for Joe's pleasure were put on hold as, hot, flustered and aroused, she gave the woman time to swish away, checked the coast was clear, then pushed a reluctant Joe outside.

Hurriedly she dragged off the dress and struggled into her own clothes, hoping she hadn't made too much noise in the exigency of the moment.

The situation didn't give her much time to think, but she managed to fix her hair and face a little before she sashayed from the fitting room with the dresses. She did her best to smooth out the red one, praying the wrinkles where it had been creased didn't shout what had transpired while she was wearing it.

Joe was waiting at the counter with his back to her, and she checked, then braced herself and strolled up to him as coolly as she could. At first she barely had the nerve to look at him. When he turned to her that hot, hungry gleam shot into his eyes and for a second her heart plunged into the mad, pulsing rhythm again, and she knew she was in trouble.

Hot, helpless trouble.

The saleswoman raised her hard, accusing gaze to Mirandi. She smoothed out each dress and examined them minutely.

Flushing, Mirandi bit her lip, careful to avoid Joe's eyes for fear of laughing. Clearly, the fitting room shenanigans had awakened suspicion.

Bracing herself, she launched into what she could at least confess without shame.

'This dress is excellent, *madame*, but I—I had a bit of trouble with the zip on this one.' She indicated the spot where the stitching had failed. 'I found it difficult to close, then I couldn't easily unzip it to take the dress off.' She illustrated as best she could with her hands.

The woman frowned suspiciously at her, examined the zip seam, then her mouth dropped open and she burst into a stream of voluble French, waving her hands in horror.

Dismayed, Mirandi turned to Joe. To her utter astonishment he took charge of the situation, addressing the saleswoman in smooth, fluent, confident French, waving his hands with Gallic expertise as if he'd been born to a chateau on the Loire. After a rapid-fire exchange of arguments, heated on the woman's side, suavely authoritative on Joe's, the woman backed down a little and a reluctant understanding appeared to be in view.

She turned to Mirandi and explained in English that perhaps the *mademoiselle* was not entirely to blame. It was possible, though extremely *unlikely*, that the fault had been with the product, as *monsieur* had pointed out.

'As it is, this dress cannot now be sold,' she declared with sly triumph. 'It must be returned to Paris and resewn.'

Joe produced a credit card and laid it smoothly before her. 'We'll take it.'

'But no, *monsieur*. This dress must not leave the shop.' The cold glint of revenge made her small black eyes harder than ever. 'As *monsieur* has stated, the reputation of our company is at stake here, of our seamstresses, of our very nation. I am afraid we cannot help *mademoiselle*.'

'I think you can, *madame*,' Joe said in a tone that, although smooth, would allow no argument. 'This is the dress we want, and it is the dress we must have. Exactly as it is. In fact, we'll take both dresses.'

Mirandi swivelled around to stare at him. 'What? *Both?*'

'Both,' he stated firmly. 'And we'll also require some matching shoes and purses.' His eyes lit on a lingerie rack in the far corner. 'And some of those lacy things with the suspenders.'

'*What?*' The shocks were coming so quick and fast Mirandi's mouth was formed in a perpetual O.

Madame considered her options for a bristling moment, then caved in. Such a profitable sale was irresistible.

Afterwards, floating along the street carrying some of the boutique's elegant packages while still more dangled from Joe's hand, Mirandi was in a giddy haze.

'Joe. I really don't know what to say—but…thank you. This was so *generous*. I mean, *two* dresses. One would be amazing enough, but *two*. And the *shoes*. And these bags are to die for. I adore them. I just *adore* them.'

He held up his hand. 'It was my pleasure. Every minute of it.' He gave a wicked reminiscent laugh.

She joined in with her own gurgle of laughter. 'All right, but you know…two—*two* dresses. Do you have any idea what those shoes cost? And two bags. I don't ever own more than one and I keep it until it falls apart. *And* those lace knickers.

And the corset with the suspenders...' She cast him a sidelong glance. 'I can't imagine where I'll ever wear that.'

'Can't you?' His eyes shimmered. 'But you are wearing it now, aren't you?' His voice was deeper than midnight.

She smiled acknowledgement. The truth was she'd admired herself in it so much, especially the way the black bustier pushed up her breasts and made them swell at the top, she hadn't been able to bear to take it off and had informed *madame* she would wear it home under her clothes.

'Clever of you to remember,' she teased.

Of course, under *madame's* watchful eye Joe hadn't been privy to the fitting room at the trying-on of the corselet, but overhearing this discussion he'd turned a fascinated gaze on Mirandi, almost as if he were seeing straight through her blue suit to the sexy black lace underneath.

'It's not the sort of thing a man forgets. It's the only thing keeping me awake.'

She laughed. 'Really. Oh, and before I forget. I have to tell you how impressed I am by your magnificent French. I've forgotten most of mine from school. For a guy who only visited France for one weekend, how do you manage it?'

He gave a shrug, and the corner of his mouth curled in a grimace. 'I once knew a Frenchwoman.'

'Oh.' Her heart took a dive. Of course. She should have known. The only question was how many?

She tried not to let it deflate her. She had no claims on him now. A fitting-room clinch didn't mark him as hers. Face it, he'd already evaded her brand of entanglement in the past. He wasn't about to plunge into it again.

Strolling along under the leafy canopy of trees, she stole a look at him and saw his face shadowed with that brooding absorption he'd had earlier, and mentally kicked herself for being a fool. Why spoil a near-perfect day with useless speculation about how many women he'd had? Was currently seeing, despite poor Kirsty having bitten the dust?

'Anyway,' she said, determined to recapture the mood. 'It was so kind and generous of you. *More* than generous, Joe, it was…' She spread her arms wide. 'How can I ever thank you?'

He grabbed her and held her still, smiling into her eyes with tender amusement. 'Don't thank me. I'm the one who should be thanking *you*.'

He put his arms around her, and, as though both driven by the same impulse, their lips collided. His strong arms tightened around her and he deepened the kiss, as far as it was possible in a public boulevard with shoppers milling around them. Straight away, so soon after the last kiss, the desire still lurking between them sprang back to life and sizzled through her like fifty thousand volts of electricity.

She'd noticed before that they were heading in the direction of the hotel and the ferry quay. When they broke apart she felt breathless and a little drunk. 'So…what do you think now? A cruise on Lake Zurich?'

His eyes shimmered. 'Well, as you said, we're jet-lagged.' His voice deepened and his expression grew solemn. 'I think an afternoon rest would do us good, don't you?' His eyes were surprisingly bright for a man contemplating sleep, his voice deep and velvety. 'Give us plenty of energy for tonight.'

'Tonight?' She sent him a quick oblique glance.

His eyes smouldered. 'Well, we don't want to waste it, do we?'

CHAPTER EIGHT

EUPHORIA was a beautiful thing. It carried them up in the lift and along the hotel corridor, punctuated by kisses and giggles from Mirandi and shouts of laughter from Joe whenever they remembered the boutique woman's face.

'We can't really blame her.'

'But at least she was happy in the end with her sale, wasn't she?'

'Though if she'd had a humane bone in her body she could at least have given us another five minutes…'

'Oh, yes, if *only*. I had *such* plans for you, you'll never know. Pity you couldn't have come in with me while I tried on the lingerie.'

Joe's eyes gleamed. 'Ah, yes. The lingerie.'

He took the key from her hand and slid it into the slot. Her room door opened, and he stood back and allowed her to float through first.

Rooms at the Chateau du Lac were airy and opulent, with windows you could open, pretty painted ceilings and a gratifying number of mirrors that gave a woman plenty of angles from which to observe the effect she was making.

She wafted into the centre of hers, twirled, then dropped her packages on the floor and turned to face Joe. Desire electrified the air, whispered along her nerve-endings and teased her erotic zones with pleasant yearning. Joe deposited his parcels on a chair, then caught her at the waist and held her still, his light firm grip searing her through her clothes.

Her breath was trapped in her lungs when she met the fever burning in his eyes like points of flame. It was too late for resolutions.

'This is exactly what we said we wouldn't do,' she said shakily, her heart pounding like a wild thing.

'And what we always knew we *would* do.'

His voice had thickened with the intensity of his lust, instantly reviving her own unassuaged desire until her body trembled to know his embrace and burned.

He reached for the top button of her jacket and she smiled as swiftly and expertly he stripped her of her suit.

His eyes flared when he revealed her in her lacy corselet. He stood back to take in the full effect of her suspenders, the stockings attached and her flimsy little see-through pants, and with a primitive urge to inspire him she slipped the grips on the suspenders and peeled off her stockings with long, caressing, sensual movements, holding each of them high and letting them flutter to the ground.

She held him at bay with a gesture, then she danced a little, provocatively stroking her hips and swaying, fanning her hair out then arching her back to let the silky stuff fall behind her in a mass.

When she straightened he was standing as though riveted, breathing hard, his eyes burning like coals. His tie was hanging loose and she saw the faintest sheen of moisture on his upper lip.

A buoyant sensation she'd nearly forgotten existed shot through her, as if her veins were injected with magic. She felt like a midnight witch, reckless and sexy and aroused. Powerful. Inspired.

Desire whispered along her nerve-endings and pulsed in her blood. Tantalising her masculine captive, she swayed a little more to help him appreciate the treasures on offer, pouted to remind him she had lips in other places, and wiggled her hips to entice him.

It seemed to work. Though she held him in check with her tease, his devouring gaze, a certain tension in the lines of his big lean body, suggested his unaccustomed patience in such a situation was about to explode into action.

She sashayed up to him to unbutton his shirt and he stood even more motionless, but it was brooding stillness like that of a ticking grenade. He watched her face while she slipped the buttons, her trembling hands affected by the powerful heartbeat she could feel beneath the thin fabric. Only his harsh quickened breath revealed the control he was employing to hold the volcano of passion in check.

He undid his cufflinks, then tore off his shirt. Her mouth dried when she saw his broad, bronzed chest again, with his powerful pecs and lean muscled abdomen as stirring as ever before. Greedily her eyes devoured the black whorls of hair arrowing down below his belt.

Sighing, unable to help herself, she pressed her lips to his hard chest and they felt scorched by the heat in his skin. At once his arms snaked around her, then his hands slid to her arms and held them in a purposeful grip. She could feel the hot current of passion flowing through him.

'I can't believe what you're doing to me,' he said, his voice deep and gravelly. 'Come here.'

He dragged her to him and seared her lips with his in masterful possession, plundering her mouth with his tongue, sucking the breath from her lungs till she was giddy, then he broke the sizzling contact to devour her throat and breasts with urgent kisses.

She struggled with the bow of her corselet but the lustful man couldn't wait for her to take it off. He lifted one breast from its cup, licked the tender yearning nipple, then drew on it with his mouth.

Oh, heavenly day. She mewled with pure pleasure, clinging

to him as her bones dissolved in bliss, then, just when she thought her desire couldn't blaze any brighter, he sucked on the other one as well, fanning the flames of her hunger to an inferno.

Fire raged through her blood and in the tender folds between her thighs until her very channel burned with longing to take him inside.

With a small growl he pushed her onto the bed, devouring her semi-nude body with his eyes while he stripped off the rest of his clothes and flung them aside.

When she saw the proud extent of his virility, her blood slowed in her veins like treacle.

'Oh, my,' she purred, moistening her lips.

There was little doubt of his enthusiasm for the task in hand. His magnificent erection jutted free and proud, and she felt her womb melt and juice dampen her between her legs in avid anticipation.

She reached out and touched him, stroking his hot, hard penis, marvelling at the velvet skin encasing the engorged beauty. Closing her hand around the shaft, she felt the roiling surge of intense heat, and, amazingly, felt him harden still further in her grasp.

'Careful,' he bit out, closing his eyes, his voice a shuddering growl.

Smiling, she rolled into the middle of the bed and lolled there with her head on the pillow, slowly parting her legs for him in voluptuous encouragement. He started in surprise, staring with his hot lubricious gaze, then deliberately leaned forward and drew her knickers off.

A shiver of excitement rippled down her spine.

He waited to see if she would resume the same enticing pose without her protective covering, and, challenged, she didn't disappoint him.

He stood smouldering, taking in her nakedness below the bustier, his eyes dark with desire, his powerful chest heaving, then all at once turned to swoop at his clothes and make a frantic search through the pockets.

With an exclamation of satisfaction he produced a foil packet and held it up, grinning.

'Aha.'

As she had so many times before, she watched him roll on the sheath, breathless with excitement for the pleasure to come.

He joined her on the bed and stretched out over her, searching her eyes hungrily at first before taking her lips in a slow tender kiss.

When he drew back she gazed up at him, feeling the fever force thrumming in his virile body, enjoying the familiar, evocative scent of him, the erotic rub of his body hair on her breasts and legs. Precious flesh on flesh, beloved bone on bone. Familiar knee, familiar hip. The old sensation that their bodies had been fashioned to fit.

He gazed at her, frowning, his eyes all at once serious. He said, a curious roughness in his deep voice, 'I can't get over how everything about you is still—with me. You're engrained in my senses.'

Her heart thrilled to hear her sensations reflected.

He added even more hoarsely, his eyes glowing with a fierce sincerity, 'I'm still wild for you. Whatever they told you, that never ended.'

His face contorted with some strong emotion, then his eyes burned with a particular primitive purpose and she tensed with expectation. She wrapped her legs around him and with a strong sure thrust he drove into her.

She let out a gasp, having forgotten how fabulously he filled her with his thick, hard length.

He scanned her face with a mesmeric, heavy-lidded gaze. 'I want to rock you until you forget every other guy in the universe.'

Breathlessly she gasped, 'What other guys?'

He started to move inside her, rocking her in a subtle, sinuous, sexy rhythm that ignited little streamlets of pleasure inside her moist, empty darkness like rays of light. He took her mouth in urgent possession, then as the rhythm grew faster and harder, and his thrusting rod stroked her aroused inner walls, she felt herself open to him. Felt the light expand as their bodies fitted, locked tight in the sexy, satisfying rumba.

She clung to her old lover as if to a lifeline, revelling in the power of him, the erotic friction with his strong chest. At first he watched her face, reading her responses, but as the tempo quickened his eyes closed and she knew he'd been overtaken by his own blissful concentration.

With each escalating thrust her pleasure soared, rising higher and higher up some steep tense slope and she was on a wild high ride to ecstasy.

She felt herself reach the summit, saw his neck sinews ridge with effort as he held back his climax to wait for her. Then just as she teetered on the edge she felt his powerful frame tense for the first spasm of climax. Somehow that violent tension fuelled her own with all the impetus she needed, and her suspense fractured and dissolved into a million exquisite shards and irradiated her entire body.

Afterwards, after she'd recovered her breath and the blood had ceased drumming in her ears, when the sweat had dried on her skin and she was free of her corselet, she turned to examine him.

He'd been up and washed, and now lay with his eyes closed, apparently dozing. The room was bathed in the soft light that preceded dusk.

'You haven't lost your touch,' she murmured.

She saw the edges of his mouth twitch. 'I know. I was inspired.'

She grinned. 'Still so charmingly modest.'

'Thank you.' His eyes opened and he reached out and touched her. '*You* inspired me.'

'Oh. Good. I hoped I was having an effect.'

'When didn't you?' He leaned towards her and kissed her lips.

That reminded her of something he'd said before about never changing, but of course he'd declared it in the heat of the moment. People often said things then. Before their brains cooled.

Still, there was a thrilling atmosphere of togetherness winding around them. He pulled her closer to him and she lay silently, pleasantly entwined, savouring the precious intimacy of afterglow, wishing it would never end.

He'd closed his eyes again, but she could tell his brain was ticking over.

'Do you still write the poems?' she said after a while, softly tracing the outline of his tattoo.

'Nope.' He smiled. 'Sometimes I think of things I might write down, and then something intervenes. You know, work... I'm surprised you remember.'

'I'm starting to remember quite a lot.'

His lips twitched. 'Not too much, I hope.' Then after a while he opened his eyes and said cautiously, 'Did you ever wish we hadn't ended when we did?'

She stilled, then disentangled herself from him and lay back on her pillow, her heart thumping ridiculously, considering it had all happened ten years ago. 'Did you?'

'I guess. Though at the time it seemed—for the best.'

A million questions jostled for answers, not least the ones beginning with 'why' if this idle conversation was intended to convey how much he regretted their crash and burn. Still, she knew how to play the caution card too. In fact, it was the only one she ever dared use these days.

'Who for?' she said, as casual as he, while underneath her façade her adolescent heart was bursting through the layers to demonstrate that all along it had been ticking away alive and well, nursing all its old unresolved violence, just waiting for a trigger, a chance to spill its guts.

His blue eyes met hers, intent, earnest, held them an intense, throat-catching instant, then veiled and slid away.

'Ah…probably both of us,' he said gruffly, retreating onto his pillow. 'It wasn't the sort of dependence either of us could afford at that age, was it?'

Spoken like a chief executive officer.

She couldn't resist some gentle mockery, unable to betray her savage soul altogether. 'You mean there was too much emotion involved? Too much passion?'

He crooked his arm over his eyes while her words floated on the air. After what seemed like for ever, he stirred himself to lean up on his elbow and gaze down at her, pure and thrilling sin brimming from his smiling eyes.

'I think we both know there can never be too much passion.' He reached for her and kissed her swollen lips with the same passionate fervour as the first time.

CHAPTER NINE

I̲T̲ ̲W̲A̲S̲ absurd to hold a grudge, and, truly, those painful emotions had long since cooled. She was an adult now, fast approaching the era of life when her womanly powers would be at their height, so if a man was fun and exciting, charming, wicked and a virile, sensitive lover who could send her over the edge, how crazy would she be to hold it against him that he'd once let her down?

So long as she kept her head and didn't harbour any destructive yearnings for a long-term arrangement, she could enjoy the current fling and walk away with a satisfied grin.

Surely.

So when the plane cruised her over the Alps and into Nice, with a night of the most fantastic and voluptuous love-making still warming her spirit she had nothing to complain of. Unless she counted a slight tenderness in certain delicate areas and a pressing need to sleep. Pity there was a day of conferencing to get through first.

To her surprise they were met at the airport by a uniformed man in a cap marked Hotel Metropole, who bowed. *'Mam'selle et monsieur,* your 'elicopter awaits you.'

'Our helicopter?' she exclaimed to Joe. 'From here into the city?'

'Oh, didn't I mention it? The conference is in Monte Carlo. *Merci,*' he said to the pilot, launching into a stream of fluent French in response to something the man said.

Monte Carlo. Well, one exotic location was as good as another, and who was she to quibble if he didn't inform her of absolutely every minute detail?

And, truly, she'd never experienced anything like that helicopter flight. It was her first time, and gazing down into the dazzling Mediterranean as it foamed up on the shores of a million little bays and inlets was a stunning experience. Marinas thronging with yachts and fishing boats, heart-stopping little villages perched on hillsides, spilling down cliff-faces... Image after charming image unfolded, etching themselves into her thrilled heart for all eternity. And Monte Carlo itself was a fairy tale. Spilling over the hillsides, the pale pink and cream sandstone city descended to a harbour marina where vessels were packed like sardines. A little further out some of the big glossy cruising yachts rode at anchor on the waves.

'You see that chateau on the edge of the sea?' their pilot enthused. 'There is our famous Monte Carlo casino. And here we go down.'

The pretty houses, the turquoise sea... Every view from every angle was breathtaking. How could Joe not be swept away?

He wasn't, though, she could tell when the fantastic ride was over and they strolled into the sumptuous lobby of the Metropole. While she glanced excitedly around her at what looked like a palace, taking in the rich furnishings, the tapestries, the elegant clientele chatting over their coffees, Joe was frowning, the grim lines around his eyes and mouth a reminder of their sleepless night.

'Why didn't you mention the helicopter and Monte Carlo?' she murmured while they were waiting for the desk clerk to attend to them.

'Maybe I don't care for the name.'

She gave him a sharp look and Joe felt a slight twinge of guilt. He supposed he had been less than forthcoming with her about the details of the trip.

'Oh, well.' He spread his hands. 'I said the south of France. There's hardly a great difference.'

'Tell that to the Monacons.'

'The Monegasque,' he corrected gently. 'Or the Monacoians.'

He could hardly blame her feeling ruffled, but the truth was the very name Monte Carlo had an unpleasant ring to him. It conjured up visions of hungry, desperate people poring over roulette wheels. Lost souls with empty eyes and wallets, risking their children's bread on the ride of a pitiless dice. Besides, the place was far too close to Antibes.

Now he was here on the spot, Antibes loomed like a black cloud. With a resurgence of that dread feeling in his gut he tried to remember why he'd allowed himself to be pressured into coming. Why hadn't he just ticked all the boxes and given the casino project the go-ahead? Did he seriously think he'd learn anything here he could use?

His vision—the one where he produced some incontrovertible evidence that changed the minds of his directors—started to look like what it was. An hallucination.

The truth was those guys were all salivating over the potential for obscene profits. Unless he could come up with an angle to quell their greed, they'd never listen.

'Joe.' He felt her tug at his sleeve. 'Which conference is ours?'

The moment of truth. Bracing for trouble, he followed Mirandi's gaze to a placard where the hotel's current conferences had been listed in both French and English.

International Bankers Symposium
Casino Acquisition and Marketing
Capital Investors Roundtable

Though his shirt collar all at once seemed to tighten around his neck like a noose, he met her gaze without flinching. 'The second.'

'Casinos? But…'

'But what?'

Wariness veiled her gaze, though he really hadn't intended that little snap in his voice.

'Well…' She gazed steadily at him. 'I guess when you mentioned entertainment for some reason I thought you meant the music industry.'

'Hardly.' He saw her brows edge together and it made his nerves jangle. 'Is there something you want to say?'

The atmosphere grew prickly. She evaded his eyes and he felt his blood pressure jump a notch. He tried to guess what she was thinking. Remembering his father, the fatal addiction? How could Joe betray his father's suffering like that? Or even worse. Was Joe the *same* as his father?

She glanced around her, extended her hands in wordless acquiescence. 'We're here, aren't we? Would anything I say make a difference?'

Irritation grabbed him. 'Probably not.'

'Then I'll save my breath.'

She flashed him a grin to show there were no hard feelings. But he could feel her slip him one or two shrewd glances. She was thinking plenty, he'd be willing to stake his last dollar on it—if he'd been a gambling man, of course, which he certainly was *not*. He could almost hear the moral judgements ticking over inside her glossy head.

Although she gave no sign of it, considering she was smiling at the desk clerk, making chit-chat with her usual serenity. Perhaps he'd misread her. Paradoxically then he regretted cutting off her queries and wished he knew exactly *what* she was thinking. One thing he could always rely on in the past was her ability to see right into the heart of an issue.

'Your keys, *mam'selle et monsieur*,' the desk clerk beamed, only too eager to assist the *mademoiselle*. 'Your baggage has already been transported to your rooms.'

Mirandi thanked him. Conscious of a need to bridge the jagged chasm suddenly yawning between her and Joe, she turned to him. 'Coffee first?' She indicated the sign pointing outside to the pool bar and café, but he glanced at his watch, frowning.

'Not if we want to unpack before we register for the conference. Don't you want to change?'

'Oh, all right.' Her heart sank. So soon? After that delightful helicopter ride, switching straight back into work mode felt something of an anticlimax, but Joe's demeanour didn't encourage rebellion.

She wished the conference was about the music industry. She wasn't sure she could bear sitting through days of discussing something that clashed with her own values and upbringing in every way. As for Joe... How could he even contemplate it?

The mood had changed. Didn't last night and the things they'd said to each other—those thrilling half-promises, all the demonstrations of rapture in each others' company—didn't they mean anything?

The upper reaches of the hotel were decorated in the same luxurious style as the vestibule, with lovely antique table lamps and paintings in unexpected corners. Whether by accident or design they'd been assigned adjoining rooms. When she reached her door she arranged to meet Joe in thirty minutes, then walked inside, frowning.

Something was wrong. She considered all the casual references Joe had made to the trip. The things he'd said in Zurich. *This bloody hell of a trip.*

Maybe it wasn't the place that was bothering him at all. Maybe it was the conference itself. She guessed that would explain his reluctance to discuss it with her.

Although what was a conference, anyway—a few meetings, a lot of discussion? Despite the topic, it was hardly something to dread. He could walk away in a minute, but he had the look of a man about to undertake some gruelling trial. Was there someone he expected to meet there he didn't want to see? Some old flame?

He had plenty of them, she thought gloomily. It wasn't hard to imagine they might pepper the world. Maybe that would explain his reluctance to share any information with her. Although…

Looking back, she realised he hadn't even been willing to tell her the theme of the conference. That hadn't just been an oversight, she could tell by the tension in his tone downstairs. Face it, it was such an *amazing* theme for Joe of all people to be exploring. Casinos, of all things.

The more she thought of it, the stranger it felt. Whoever he was now, she knew the Joe he'd been and where he'd come from. One thing she remembered all too clearly was his dislike of casinos and all their implications.

And it was understandable, for him. He might not have been brought up as she had by a tough church minister with a tender social conscience, but as a teenager he'd been dealt one of life's cruellest blows.

Joe had put the tragedy behind him, but Jake had been his father, his beloved father, and though Joe never spoke of that terrible time she knew it was woven into the fabric of him, warp and weft. In fact, anyone knowing these things about Joe would assume Monte Carlo to be the last place he'd think of visiting.

So why had he chosen to come?

Worriedly, she turned her attention to locating her suitcase, and for the first time took time to examine her room properly.

Overwhelmed, she stood stock still to drink it all in.

After the luxury of Zurich she knew better than to wonder if Stella had made some mistake with the bookings. This time the thoughtful woman had excelled herself.

The room was charming, opulent and distinctly French. High of ceiling, it boasted an antique writing desk and rose satin drapes framing two sets of French doors that opened to a small balcony.

Unable to resist, Mirandi walked outside and leaned on the stone balustrade, inhaling the heady Mediterranean air, thrilled by the sights and sounds of the fairy-tale city. Below her was a terraced garden with ponds and fountains and beyond that, across the rooftops, the sea.

If only she and Joe were here on a real holiday. She toyed with the idea of distracting him from his purpose. Considerations of how she might achieve it would have made her grin if she hadn't felt such a sense of foreboding. His moods had suddenly become so unpredictable who knew if he'd still want her by nightfall?

With a sigh she turned back inside.

If she had to be confined to a hotel, she was glad it was this one, at any rate.

She strolled around, opening all the doors and investigating the drawers.

The king-sized bed—surely an excess for one person—was attired with a heavy satin counterpane of roses on a cream background, with rose-covered pillows. A vase of the real thing in fragrant, partly unfurled buds of pink and red adorned a side table.

It was a duchess's room. A princess's. She couldn't wait to sink amongst those fluffy pillows on that inviting bed and sleep.

The bathroom was equally grand. Besides vast expanses of marble and a glassed-in shower recess, she was gratified to find a huge old-fashioned tub with detachable shower hose. Beside it, fresh rose petals in a jar waited to float in her bath water.

Perfect. Or it would be, once the conference was finished for the day.

She sighed again, and set about hanging up her clothes. At least Joe had given her the two lovely dresses and she wouldn't be disgracing herself among the glamorous clientele. The minor problem of that tricky zip occurred to her, and, taking up the brochure detailing the hotel facilities, she sprawled as delicately as she could on the rose-covered counterpane and leafed through it.

Aha. As she'd hoped, garment mending was on offer. Taking a chance the person on the other end of the phone had better English than her few words of French, she dialled Housekeeping. In no time a housemaid was at the door to collect her red dress with the promise it would be hanging back in the closet within the hour.

This was the life.

She changed into her suit and was brushing her hair when Joe's crisp tap sounded on the door. Conference time.

Joe had definitely switched into CEO mode, his eyes serious and purposeful, the lines of his face taut. She grimaced. Forget any notions of a holiday. This was business.

Downstairs, they queued at the conference desk among all the other business people with their briefcases and phones. She was frowning into space, trying to remember what else Auntie Mim had told her about Jake Sinclair, when Joe suddenly took her hand and gave it a squeeze.

'Don't look so worried.' He gave her a wry smile. 'It's only the jaws of hell we're walking into.'

She grinned, her heart glowing with relief. He was still there somewhere, her tender, mocking, affectionate Joe.

Once they'd signed in and been issued with ID tags and prospectuses, he suggested they plan their agenda over coffee by the pool. Mirandi needed no persuading.

They waited for their coffees seated in comfortable armchairs on the pool terrace. The pool looked almost too inviting to resist, with its radiant aqua water lapping the tiles at its edge. The sun dappled their table, a sea-scented breeze trifled with her hair, and while she perused the conference agenda she was half aware of the holiday tang of sun lotion, splashes and shouts of laughter from people with nothing to do but play.

There were information sessions planned all that day and the next with a cocktail party to be held at the casino that evening. She read that delegates would have an opportunity to try their luck at the tables, if they so desired. She pursed her lips, frowning.

Delegates. People like her and Joe.

No one would come to Monte Carlo without visiting the casino, at least for a look. Even her father would be interested in visiting the building to view its fabled splendours. So why did she feel so uneasy?

She scoured her conscience, aware of a nasty gnawing sensation in the pit of her stomach. Admit it. She didn't want Joe to go there. Everything about it seemed so—dangerous. What if…? A frightening thought crossed her mind and she crushed it to smithereens.

That wouldn't be Joe. It just wouldn't.

A waiter brought their coffees and placed them on the low table between them.

Though who ever knew they had a weakness until opportunity crossed their path? A sickening thought crept up on her. Maybe the addiction had already claimed him. Wouldn't that explain the entire trip?

'Well, out with it,' Joe said, replacing his wallet after slipping the man a note. 'I'm sure you have an opinion.'

Mirandi glanced up warily from stirring her coffee. 'About what?'

'You know what.'

She raised the cup to her lips and sipped the creamy brew, then glanced across at him. His expression was apparently relaxed, but his black brows were drawn over his alert blue eyes and there was a curious tension in his frame, as if the fate of the world suddenly hung on her reply.

What could she say? Don't risk it, Joe? Turn away from temptation before it sucks you in like quicksand?

She gave a shrug. 'The hotel is fabulous, my room is a

dream. I have a lovely dress to wear tonight and another one tomorrow night. I'm jet-lagged and a little tired and would appreciate a long hot soak in that tub upstairs, but you're the boss. If you say I have to spend my time on the Côte d'Azur in a conference about gaming, then that's what I'll do.'

His mouth tightened. 'I get it. You disapprove, but you're just following orders.'

She blinked, startled. 'What do you want me to say?'

Anger flashed from his eyes. 'Be honest. Say what you think.'

Hot words rushed to her tongue but she bit them back. 'I'm a market analyst for an investment company, remember? Too much sensibility is a handicap for the likes of me.'

'That's no answer and you know it. It's a cop-out.'

The unexpected emotional undertow was dragging her towards saying some things she might regret. But she held her cup tight and kept her voice cool. 'If you're planning on investing in a casino I'm sure it will be very lucrative. I'm not your conscience.'

'Good,' he said curtly, rising to his feet. He pointed a warning finger. 'Just you remember that.'

But…but…what had she said? Her head swirling with bewilderment and annoyance, she followed him back inside.

'Well, anyway,' she said, hurrying to keep up with him as he strode towards the lift. 'Thousands of people go to casinos every day without coming to any harm. Millions. People are free to choose their style of entertainment. If rich people want to play games with their money…'

He halted and turned fiercely on her, grabbing her arm. '*Don't* say that to me. Don't *ever*…' His face twisted and she was shaken by a bolt of utter shock. He must have seen it because he released her arm and brought his momentary loss of cool under control. 'Sorry. I'm sorry. But—*don't* try preaching morality as per the blessed Reverend Summers at me, either. I'm here to make a reasoned decision. *You're* here as an MA, so stay out of it.'

She blinked. 'But what have I said? All I said was... You *asked* me...'

He made a stern silencing gesture.

Fuming, she folded her arms and turned her back on him on the ride up in the lift. Fine, not another word on the subject would cross her lips. If his conscience was so tender, let him deal with it on his own.

Not surprisingly, the conference sessions were an endurance. With Joe so apparently angry with her for no good reason, she felt too resentful to care if he gleaned any useful information from the various speakers with all their videos and graphs and risk projections. She listened to it all on one level and brooded on another.

Every so often she felt his eyes flick to her as if attempting to penetrate her reactions to the topics under discussion. Things about profit. Loss. Public relations. She refused to help him out. If he didn't know what she really thought of it all, then he didn't know Mirandi Summers.

He didn't recover his good humour. During the lunch break, while other delegates took the opportunity to meet each other and engage in civilised conversation on the terrace, he leaned up against the stonework looking like a thundercloud, his arms folded across his chest.

She supposed it didn't help that the roof of the casino was visible through the shrubbery, the dome and spires of the fanciful Belle Epoque extravaganza drawing admiring comments from the gathering. Luring them there.

Joe remained silent. She attempted conversation a few times but he was as impenetrable as a wall and she gave up. She'd have had no one to talk to at all if a pleasant American man hadn't started up a conversation with her when she sashayed over for a refill of her coffee.

He introduced himself as Louis. He was from Chicago.

A lawyer, he told her in his charming American drawl. He looked smooth and clever and had twinkling dark eyes and a way of looking at a woman as if she were the only person in the world. In truth, he seemed quite intrigued by her accent.

Naturally she warmed to him. She might have laughed once or twice at some of the teasing things he said about Aussies, because once she glanced over at Joe and was nearly electrocuted by his forbidding blue glare.

The sheer nerve of the guy. He wouldn't talk to her *himself*, but he didn't want her to chat with anyone else.

It was a relief to meet such an uncomplicated, friendly guy as Louis. She turned her back on Joe Sinclair, though her insides were churning with hurt and resentment at his unreasonable behaviour, and she could feel his eyes boring through the back of her skull.

Louis took out his phone and showed her pictures of himself competing in a swimming race in Lake Michigan. The event was called Big Shoulders, and the photos proved Louis had the shoulders, all right. And the chest. There was nothing wrong with his abs, either.

She was just leaning over to delve further when Joe strode up, brusquely introduced himself, shook Louis's hand in what looked like a crushing grip, then hustled her back inside the hotel.

'We need to go through our notes,' he stated.

'What notes would that be?' she snapped. 'I'm not aware you took any.'

'But you did, surely. Surely I can rely on you for *something*.'

'Well, no, you can't. I'm out of it, remember? Boss's orders.'

He closed his eyes briefly. 'Mirandi...' He made some kind of effort and the rigidity of his shoulders eased. All at once he looked so weary her heart melted with pity for him.

'Look.' He breathed deeply, his hands clenching and

unclenching. 'I'm not really in the mood for games. Try to be less provocative, will you?'

The sheer injustice of the man. She abandoned her sympathy and raised a haughty eyebrow. 'That will be hard for a woman of my renowned temperament, Joe. In fact, at the risk of being provocative, I think you're seriously overtired. If you ask me anything, you should be spending this afternoon sleeping.'

'Then it's as well I'm not asking you, isn't it?' he said in a gentle, maddeningly reasonable voice.

Hostilities didn't improve during the afternoon, although there weren't more actual words spoken. When the last interminable session ended, she and Joe stalked to the lifts to join the small crowd waiting there in stony silence.

At last there was a ping, then one set of lift doors slid open to eject a small party of women. As they emerged into the hall, chattering and laughing, one small elderly lady in the middle of the bunch suddenly stopped and stood stock still, staring.

Her face seemed to stiffen. *'Joseph.'*

Whipping a surprised glance at Joe, Mirandi saw that he seemed to have frozen still. But he was only disconcerted for a moment. Before her eyes his face smoothed into an expressionless mask.

'I'm afraid I don't know you, *madame*,' he said to the small woman, utterly chilling in his politeness. Mirandi became aware then of his grip tightening to steel on her arm and being jostled in to join the crowd in the lift.

Just before the doors closed Mirandi saw the woman halt and turn for another glimpse of them, her eyes huge in her white face.

Mirandi rubbed her arm resentfully. Conscious of the others in the small space with them, she lowered her voice. 'Who was—?'

She broke off when she glanced at Joe.

His posture had taken on a strange rigidity. His jaw was

tight—clenched, his nostrils flaring, while his eyes glittered like ice beneath his black brows. She noted with a small shock a tiny vein throbbing in his temple.

Whatever the small woman represented to Joe Sinclair, it was dynamite.

The lift stopped at their floor and they had to wait their turn to exit. As soon as they were in the hall and out of earshot of other people, she ventured to Joe, 'Are you all right?'

'What do you mean? Of course I'm *all right*.' He didn't sound all right. He reefed his hand distractedly through his hair, then made an apologetic gesture. 'Sorry. What was that you were saying? Oh, and, er…sorry about earlier. I know I've been a bit… It's been a long forty-eight hours. How about you? Are *you* all right?'

Hang on. Was she in some parallel universe? Unless her radar was way out of whack something tumultuous had just happened to Joe, and here he was talking as if she'd enquired about the weather. Though smooth enough, he couldn't disguise the unnaturalness in his tone, or the effort it was taking to produce those normal-sounding words.

Whatever the encounter meant, clearly he wasn't about to discuss it with her. Well, Mirandi Summers could take a hint. Curiosity might be killing her, but she was beginning to guess when not to intrude. Though the way things had gone for her this day she could be wrong.

Following his lead, she acted as though nothing unusual had occurred in the vestibule of the Hotel Metropole, and continued on with the artificial small talk.

Like a tightrope dancer pirouetting on point across Niagara Falls she said, 'Truthfully? I'm shattered. I can't wait to sink into a hot tub. Are you—are you planning on going to the casino tonight?'

He'd stopped to stare fixedly at a painting in the hall. It was an oil, a view of a local fishing village.

When he didn't reply she repeated her question, and

he swung around all at once to laser her with a glittering glance. He said very softly, 'Is there any reason you think I shouldn't?'

With a stab of guilt she struggled to retrieve herself. 'Well, no. Not at all. I just wondered if—since we're both quite tired...' Suddenly everywhere she turned was a no-go zone with an elephant galumphing all over it.

'Don't you want to go?' he demanded.

'Look,' she said, clenching her fists at her sides. 'I'm happy to go if you want to.'

'You really want to?' He narrowed his eyes searchingly at her.

She hesitated. '*If* you want me to.' She smiled in hopeful appeal. 'Or maybe you'd prefer to go another time when we're better rested.'

'No, I wouldn't,' he muttered grimly. 'All right then. Let's do it and get the whole bloody thing over with.' Then he seemed to collect himself a little. 'I mean, this is an important part of the whole event. We need to immerse ourselves in it to get the full picture.'

'Oh, Joe.' She rolled her eyes and couldn't help muttering to herself. 'As if you don't *know* what the full picture is.'

But his gaze had drifted back to the painting and it didn't seem to matter what she muttered, because it was pretty clear he wasn't hearing a word she was saying.

Eventually he stirred himself to move on and they reached her room. She unlocked the door, then turned to him. She cleared her throat.

'Joe, who was that woman in the lobby?'

He closed his eyes. 'No one. You know, Mirandi, you should—never give into jet-lag. It's best to carry on regardless until you drop.' He pushed back his cuff and showed her his watch. 'See? It's barely five.'

She hardly took in the time. All she could focus on was Joe's hand, shaking. Joe, the coolest, strongest, most controlled guy she'd ever met. He must have noticed it at the same time because he drew back his hand and said harshly, 'All right? I'll collect you in two hours.'

Two hours were hardly the time she needed for a decent wallow, a satisfying snooze and time to dress, but somehow she didn't feel like pushing him any further. 'Look, are you sure you're—?'

'What?' he said sharply.

'Oh, nothing. Two hours, then.'

Left to her own devices, she stood chewing her lip, speculating on the woman downstairs. The Frenchwoman.

Joe closed his door behind him and headed straight for the minibar. Thank God for single malt.

He downed a quick Scotch, then another. Somewhere through the third his heartrate slowed down to a gallop and his blood pressure felt as if it was beginning to subside. He made the effort to think.

He'd probably laugh later—much later—at the amazing irony. Of all the traps set by fate, this had to be the most diabolical. Now that the woman had sprung his presence here, she'd seek him out again, that much was certain. She'd hound him and harass him… Just as she had when he was a boy. After the funeral. As if he could ever have borne to lay eyes on her again.

Some dark injustice he was doing her clawed inside his chest but he ignored it. He'd check them out of the hotel tomorrow, first thing. Take the first flight they could catch. Mirandi had seemed enchanted with Zurich, though *anywhere*, anywhere would do. He could explain to her that the conference was too…too…

Oh, bloody hell. The board. His shareholders.

He felt moisture on his hand and looked down in surprise. Somehow the glass had broken and blood mixed with whisky was dripping from his fingers onto the floor. He glanced around for the bathroom and strode for a wash cloth.

Lucky the cut was little more than a scratch. Wrapping his hand in the cloth, he caught sight of himself in the mirror and did a double take. His heart muscle suffered another slam. Was that *him*? He looked like a guy who'd seen a ghost.

Forcing himself to breathe, he acknowledged he had, in a manner of speaking. He was a million miles from the guy in that Zurich mirror early this morning. Anyone seeing him now would think he was falling apart.

His gut clenched. Mirandi would think it. Those green eyes saw too much.

He felt an urgent, almost irresistible yearning to go in there at once, talk to her, be with her, lose himself in her. Chat about ordinary things. Make sexy small talk. Tease her and enjoy the shock in her eyes when he said something wicked. Drown in her smiling gaze. Lay his head on her soft, forgiving breasts and sleep for a hundred years.

He was actually shaking. He recognised with disbelief that he was teetering on the verge of a loss of control. He needed to get a grip. Shock must have momentarily thrown him, that was all.

He took a deep breath and leaned both hands on the vanity to steady himself. Remember your forte, Sinclair, he commanded himself. Compartmentalise. Stuff all the horrors back into their appropriate boxes and batten down the lids.

He wasn't a shell-shocked kid any more and if he could hold the past at bay *then*, he could more than do it now. Amelie Sinclair had no power to affect him. Amelie Sinclair…that little woman…

How small she'd seemed. Could she have shrunk?

He tried to calculate how old she'd be now. She was certainly showing her age. The lines beneath her eyes had deepened and multiplied. She'd looked—harmless.

Of course she was *harmless*, for God's sake. She was merely…merely…

In a determined effort to relax, he loosened his shoulders and breathed out. Concentrate on the good things. A shower, shave, and—he flinched away from thinking about the cocktail function. The casino had to be faced, though, and, admit it, he had some curiosity about the place.

It was more than time he set foot inside a casino and tested his mettle, and why not this one? After all, it was where his father had first contracted his addiction. Surely if he hadn't succumbed by now he never would. People couldn't inherit *all* their parents' genes.

He'd endure it as long as he could, then once that hurdle was past he could relax with Mirandi over dinner, and, if there truly was a God, hold her lusciousness in his arms all night and sink into blessed forgetfulness and release.

Though come to think of it, Mirandi had been astoundingly difficult all day long. Nothing had shocked or shamed her. Anyone would think she *loved* casinos. Of all the people in the world he'd thought he could rely on…

Shouldn't she be trying to talk him out of it?

A man believed he knew a woman, understood her through to her bone marrow, knew where he was with her, knew exactly what to expect from her, then the minute he took his eyes from her for a year or so she morphed into another being altogether.

If only all bathtubs came with padded neck rests. Still, the water was as hot as she could bear it, and Mirandi sank into it by degrees and relaxed.

Ah-h-h. She lay back and closed her eyes, luxuriating, thinking of Joe, running the day's conversations through her mind like a tape. It seemed to her that just about everything she'd said today had irritated him. She couldn't remember ever seeing Joe in this cantankerous mood. The guy was spoiling for a fight.

She closed her eyes, but it was hard to hold onto thoughts

with this tingling warmth permeating her bones all the way up to her chin. The sensual pleasantness lulled her into a dreamy state somewhere between a stupor and sleep until the water began to chill, then suddenly, from out of nowhere, a jarring thought pierced the mists.

Her eyes sprang open and she sat bolt upright.

If a man grew tired of a woman's company, a man suffering the effects of jet-lag and in the grip of a terrible fascination, might it not be difficult for that man to conceal his boredom and irritation? Considering they'd been in close confinement now for more than forty-eight hours, wasn't it almost inevitable that Joe *should* be fed up with her?

Was this simply a case of history repeating itself?

Now that he'd had her and achieved his victory, it wasn't impossible he'd tired of her all over again. With a nasty stab she remembered only too clearly the suddenness of his turn-around in feeling the last time. Loved and desired one day, consigned to the deep freeze the next.

With increasing desperation she scrolled through the day's events. This morning she'd been riding high, floating on a cloud of rose petals buoyed up by the warmth and intimacy of the night in his arms. Then as soon as they checked into this hotel…

Briefly she closed her eyes, then dragged herself out of the tub.

That peach and rose dress was lovely, but was lovely enough? Would that dress cut it? Maybe she needed hot, sexy and exciting.

Whatever it took, she'd glide like a goddess tonight if it killed her.

CHAPTER TEN

MIRANDI'S nerves were strung tight by the time Joe's knock sounded on her door, but she'd done her best with her appearance. At least she'd go down fighting.

She'd twisted her hair into a chignon and hadn't spared either the mascara, the eyeshadow or the ruby-red lipstick. The impossibly high stilettos from the boutique in Zurich lengthened her legs and made her appear tall and magically slender. She didn't have any diamonds, but a pendant on a silver chain drew the eye to her plunging neckline.

If she looked like something of a femme fatale, the long, worldless glance Joe razed her to the floor with when she nervously opened the door to him put at least one of her fears to flight.

In truth, his eyes riveted to her in much the same way as they had the day before in the fitting room. Her other fears weren't vanquished so quickly.

When she surveyed him looking ruggedly handsome in his beautiful dinner suit with the snowy evening shirt and black tie, she had to wonder if he was used to visiting casinos. He would fit in only too perfectly.

At the same instant she realised that despite feeling so troubled she was in deep herself, all over again. Right back where she'd been ten years ago, in the grip of an obsession with Joe Sinclair. Whatever he was, she wanted him. Madly. Absolutely. He smelled so delicious with that appealing tang of fresh, masculine shower essences. In spite of everything, drinking in the smooth kissability of his lean, tanned cheek, she could have eaten him alive on the spot.

As if he felt the current his hot gaze connected with hers, then he grabbed her right there in the doorway and dragged her up against him, searing her lips and every cell in her body in a hot, sexy kiss, tongues and all.

The clinch could have escalated to so much more if people hadn't swished by outside at that exact moment, reminding them of where they were supposed to be going.

They broke apart, and she was left reeling and aroused.

'At least that hasn't changed,' he said, his voice thick and gravelly. He touched a white handkerchief to his mouth. 'You'd better fix your lipstick.'

'Thanks,' she panted quite hoarsely, knowing her pupils were probably as dilated as his. 'I'll do that. You know you— taste of whisky.'

'Do I? *You* taste like nectar.'

Sensing a truce, she smiled and fluttered her lashes. 'And you look like James Bond.'

That might have been a bridge too far. He winced and she tensed, hoping he didn't explode. But he merely continued to scour her with hot sensual appreciation, growling, 'And you look *amazing*.'

On the bright side, whatever had rattled him about the Frenchwoman seemed to have smoothed away, though he carried an air of grim tension about him. His eyes were flint hard and he had a sort of coiled purpose.

As they paused in the queue before the grand entrance to the casino to search for their passes she felt him brace as for an ordeal. When it was their turn, she tucked her hand into the crook of his arm and glided in beside him.

Her first overwhelming impression, apart from the dazzling

chandeliers, was the buzz of the place. Strains of an orchestra reached them and it was impossible not to be infected by a thrilling pulse of excitement in the air.

Cocktails were served in the atrium. 'Oh, Joe,' she exclaimed when they entered the magnificent marble hall. 'Oh, look. It *is* a gilded palace. It really is.'

She spun around to gaze at the glorious ceilings, adorned with gold leaf and frescoed paintings high above a gallery supported by ionic columns. Off to one side of the salon an orchestra played.

Quite a large assembly of delegates to the conference had chosen to attend, and the salon was crowded with people in evening dress. After a short interval one of the conference hosts stepped up onto a dais at one end with a little speech of welcome, inviting them all to enjoy the drinks and the music, dance a little, dine in any of the restaurants and visit any of the public rooms.

In spite of her gnawing anxiety all at once she felt eager to see as much as she could of this jewel of the Belle Epoque.

Joe surveyed the beautiful salon with a serious gaze. 'My father came here as a young man. He was in love with the architecture of the place.' He made a grimace. 'Unfortunately it wasn't the architecture that stayed with him.'

Startled, she looked quickly at him. He'd rarely ever spoken of his father, never of his addiction, and she found this unexpected openness heartening.

A waiter materialised beside them with a tray of drinks. After a moment's hesitation Mirandi accepted a tall flute of champagne. Accepting one himself, Joe turned a surprised gaze on her.

'I'd thought you didn't indulge.'

'I do sometimes.'

'But haven't you made some sort of vow?' He looked almost

disapproving, frowning from her to her guilty glass, and she was aware of a tiny spurt of annoyance.

She smiled tightly. 'Listen to you. You sound like Auntie Mim.'

'I'm shocked, that's all.'

He sipped his own wine, glancing absently about at the guests without apparently noticing his glaring double standard. Then he turned back to her.

'You didn't drink on the plane.'

She shrugged.

'Or in Zurich.'

'I don't enjoy drinking on planes. I didn't feel like wine in Zurich. I was high enough.' She lifted her eyebrows. 'Remember?'

'But…' His jaw hardened and, like a mastiff worrying a bone, he shook his head. 'In the apartment the other afternoon you said…I'm *sure* you said…'

She stared at him in surprise. 'What? That I don't drink during working hours? For goodness' sake, Joe, does it matter?'

'No, no. It's just that…I guess I'm surprised. I keep expecting you to be…'

'What? *Perfect?*' She rolled her eyes, then conscious she might have seemed to be overreacting a tad, pasted on a smile. 'Sorry.' She gave his arm a pat. 'I'm afraid it's too late. I broke my non-alcohol rule years ago. In your presence, if you remember.'

He shook his head. 'Yeah, but…'

But. Always a but.

She laughed, though the truth was her neck was growing hot and she was beginning to feel irritated. So she'd broken her pledge. Millions did it. Face it, in her father's eyes she was a sinner and hellfire awaited her. She had her moments of discomfort about that, but it was her problem. What was *wrong* with the man?

'I'm sure you didn't ever drink very much,' he went on, warming to his theme. 'You couldn't take more than a glass, as I recall.'

'Still can't really. I hope you're not *too* disappointed at how I've turned out.' Like the loose woman she was, she gave her champagne a slurp then ran her tongue-tip provocatively over her top lip. 'I'll try to improve later and be the Miss Goody-Two-Shoes of your imagination.'

She was relieved then to see his eyes gleam with their usual one-track wickedness. He slipped his arm around her and brushed her ear with his lips. 'Not *too* good, I hope. I *like* the way you've turned out.'

Oh, he smelled so fantastically male. Still, it took her a few minutes to quite lose that prickly feeling. She was starting to feel as if she had competition. The Mirandi Summers of ten years ago must have left quite an impression.

Perhaps affected by the dazzle of their legendary surroundings and assisted by French champagne, the dull bankers and business people of the conference had acquired some sparkle to match their pretty jewellery. As the waiters circulated among them with trays laden with drinks and hors d'oeuvres, the conversation rose to a hum and she and Joe found themselves drawn into a circle of bankers and billionaires and their partners.

As she might have expected here of all places, the conversation was mainly about the play. Some of the people were keen to share their experiences at the tables, while others remained silent and watchful.

Joe was one of the silent ones, listening and absorbing, and Mirandi felt her unease increase. This wasn't a good place for Joe, among these people. Too many skeletons were present. Too many seductive influences.

She wished she could just relax, and that she and Joe could be like all those other couples who were here on a night out.

Laughing, dining and dancing, then going home and making love without any anxieties and undercurrents.

She glanced at him, so darkly handsome in his dinner suit, and her entire being clenched with yearning. Why was it that the more barriers she sensed between them, the more she wanted him?

Dancing was under way. A few couples at first, then more as the tempo of the party gathered pace. At one stage she saw Louis from Chicago pushing a statuesque blonde around the dance floor.

'How about it?' she suggested brightly, tilting her head towards the dancers.

Joe made a grimace. 'I'm not really in the mood. Later, maybe?'

Fine. She wasn't desperate to be held in anyone's arms. Other people began to drift towards the salons where the games were under way, so she and Joe followed, strolling from room to room, gazing at the magnificent decor and artwork in each unique space. She couldn't really enjoy it. After the dancing rejection her confidence had started to slip, and she was too burningly aware of the groups riveted by the action at the tables. In some of those grand salons the air fairly crackled with suspense.

If she was so aware of the allure of those tables, how must Joe feel?

They paused at a roulette table and remained there for minutes, mesmerised. The croupier called for a halt to the bids and, as one, the gamblers hunched, poised over the wheel with avid eyes, their adrenaline almost palpable in the air. When the wheel stopped spinning and the ball rolled to its final resting place, all but one set of shoulders slumped a little. A pile of chips was raked towards the flushed, radiant young guy who was the winner, while others at the table watched with hooded gazes, then prepared to place more bids, hunger in their eyes.

She couldn't deny the hypnotic pull of the game and began to feel almost hypersensitive to the tension she'd sensed in Joe ever since their descent into Monte Carlo. Was the fever in this room infecting his blood?

He turned towards her and she could feel him watching her, assessing her reactions. Though he appeared so smooth and controlled, she sensed some subterranean current churning in him, despite his genial responses. She felt a sudden, almost desperate impulse to drag him to some non-threatening place where they could just be natural and open with each other and pretend the past had never happened.

She made an attempt to draw him away, tugging at his sleeve. 'Why don't we…? How about we have dinner somewhere in the city? There were some interesting restaurants on the other side of the hotel.'

His eyes glinted. 'Why not here?' Her heart sank as she read the almost sardonic amusement in his gaze. 'Not enough action for you, or too much?' His sudden piercing glance penetrated her suspicious soul like a laser beam. 'Are you feeling uncomfortable here, Mirandi?'

She flushed. 'No, not at all. I'm sure *here* would be fantastic, though without having booked a table…' She swallowed as she heard the lameness of the excuse. 'Do you think we'd have much chance?' His quizzical brows lifted higher and she hastened to add, 'I mean it would be terrific if we *could*. Heavens—it's so sophisticated. I'm sure every restaurant here must be—wonderful. Everything's—so—so—elegant. The chefs probably have Michelin stars coming out of their ears. I'm sure they're probably booked out every night of the week. People from all over must come here…'

When she finally ran out of assurances he said gently, 'Let's put it to the test, shall we?'

Great. She'd talked him into the very thing she wanted to avoid. And just her luck, a smooth and efficient maître d'hotel found them a table at once in Le Train Bleu, a restaurant atmospherically decorated to resemble a gracious wagon-lit of the thirties.

The food might have been superb, but she failed to do hers justice. Green risotto with chanterelle mushrooms was certainly delicious, whether or not real snails had been sacrificed to create it, but it required a woman with a calm and confident stomach to dig in with gusto, and hers was anything but.

Instead she drank more wine, perhaps a little defiantly. She kept glancing at Joe when she sipped to see how her indulgence in the stuff was affecting him, but though he looked at her from time to time his expression remained impassive.

Somehow the more she worried, the more Joe exuded calm and composure. He tucked into his filet with enthusiasm, and finished up all her leftovers, including the truffled potatoes and the tarte de citron she'd optimistically ordered for dessert.

At the end of the meal when the bill was paid and the coffees nearly empty, she said, 'Shall we go back to the hotel? Have an early night?'

'First I think we should try our luck at the tables.'

Her heart plummeted, and she couldn't restrain herself from bursting out, 'Oh, Joe, *why*?'

'Why not?' He was scrutinising her, a curious light in his eyes. 'Since we're here, it seems silly not to taste the experience.'

She stared at him in appeal, imploring him with everything she could bring to bear. 'But…I can't do that. You know I can't.'

'Why not? Live dangerously. Take a walk on the wild side. Isn't that what you love?'

'Well…' She closed her eyes. '*No*— Look, it probably sounds uncool, but…' The words were dredged out of her. 'Don't mock, but you know I once made a promise. This is the one I *can't* break.' He smiled and started to speak but she hastened on. 'Try to understand.' Visions assailed her of all those sad people her father had brought home in the early hours. Knocks on the door in the dead of night. Broken, desperate people with nowhere else to turn. 'After—after all those years my father worked at the shelter… Then in Lavender Bay… All those poor people he's helped…'

Joe's blue gaze held hers, then he said drily, 'I think you're thinking of *my* father.'

She gazed wordlessly at him, then lowered her eyes. 'Yes.'

A silence fell between them, deeper than the deepest gully on the Mediterranean floor. Then he said in a quiet, level tone, 'I'm not mocking. You see, this is *my* challenge. I don't want you to participate if it hurts you. If you don't want to stay I'll take you back to the hotel.'

Her heart thudded and she squeezed her hands together. 'But, Joe, I… Must you? Do you really have to do it?'

'Believe it.' He regarded her with an intent, shimmering gaze for seconds, then he rose. 'Come on. I'll take you home first and you won't have to watch.'

She stood up and grabbed her purse. '*Oh*, I can see you're already sucked in.' Her throat had thickened and made her voice croakier than a frog's. 'Do you know what? You're a fool, Joe Sinclair.'

She marched out ahead of him, as far as it was possible to march in a skintight dress and very high heels. He attempted to steer her towards the entrance, but she snapped, her eyes swimming all at once, 'No, I'm not leaving. I intend to stay and watch the whole ghastly catastrophe.'

He broke into a grim laugh. 'Now who's talking like Auntie Mim?'

Then, true to his mad intent, ignoring all her pleading and the common sense he was born with, he headed for the salon where he'd already been hypnotised by the roulette wheel.

CHAPTER ELEVEN

MIRANDI only watched for a minute or two after Joe joined the crowd at the roulette table. It was too painful to see him ignore everything she'd said, exchange his precious hard-earned cash for chips, push a stack of them onto a square marked out in the green baize, then concentrate all his brilliance on a spinning wheel.

Instead, she retreated to the bar, commandeered one of the elegant bar stools and focused her blurry gaze on the bartender, whose white dinner jacket set off his Mediterranean tan and flashing dark eyes to perfection. If she tilted her head to the right she could just see Joe's back reflected in the mirror behind the bar, but she couldn't bear to look too often.

She ordered a flirtini with a squirt of pomegranate juice, and anguished. This could be the start of Joe's slide into ruin right here and now, and what good was she? When the chips were down, she could only look on, wailing and gnashing her teeth. What if he was so hooked she couldn't drag him away for days? Weeks even?

It was a disaster, but she couldn't help feeling some indignation towards him. He'd told her he wanted her along as a friend, his sounding board, but the minute she gave him some friendly advice he flung it back in her teeth. Accusing her of sounding like Auntie Mim when all she was trying to do was to save him from himself.

Auntie Mim indeed. She was as far from being like Auntie

Mim as it was possible to get. Ever since they'd arrived in Monte Carlo she'd bent over backwards to go with the flow and not lecture him, when the truth was… When what she secretly ached to do… *Someone* should tell him the truth.

Here she'd been secretly beaming and hugging herself about being back together with him. Admit it, she'd been wishing and hoping as the song said. Praying their relationship would stick this time round. Believing that since they'd grown up they could behave towards each other like adults.

Why did the past always have to dog their footsteps?

She dabbed at her eyes with a tissue, wishing she had the physical strength to march over there, grab Joe by the scruff and haul him out, away from the bitter influences of his past and into the twenty-first century.

The flirtini was honey smooth, and she was halfway through it when someone strolled up and parked on the bar stool second along from hers. She glanced up into the mirror and saw it was Louis.

Without appearing to notice her presence, although how he could have missed her was the biggest mystery since the pyramids, he ordered a whisky. Sporting the traditional evening wear and having allowed his beard to make an interesting stubble, he still wasn't looking quite as chipper as he'd been at the lunch. In truth, he looked a little the worse for wear, and he was frowning into his Scotch as if he had something on his mind.

Perhaps the blonde hadn't worked out. Pity, but everyone in the world had problems. It was a bittersweet symphony, right?

After a while he turned her way and gave a stagey little start as if seeing her there was a complete surprise, then made a long, slow and very comprehensive survey. He took a meditative sip of his drink.

'That's some dress.'

'Thanks.'

He gave his eyebrows a seductive tilt. 'You know, you're a very lovely woman.'

'That's what Joe says.'

On another occasion she might have enjoyed crushing Louis' pretensions with a little robust repartee, but right at this minute, with Joe embarking on a life of misery and decadence, she felt too lacklustre to rise to her usual heights.

Perhaps Louis heard the listlessness in her tone, because he swivelled his stool around until he was facing her. 'Oh, you mean Tough Guy. You know, I noticed you the minute you walked in with him.'

'And I'm sure he noticed you noticing.'

He grinned in acknowledgement of her warning shot, flashing his perfect American teeth. Then he nodded his head and sighed. 'What is it with chicks? They make themselves gorgeous for a guy and all he's interested in is a little ball rolling around a wheel.'

That struck a nerve, but she tried not to show it. Forced herself not to even blink or wring her hands, though she wanted to severely. 'He's just trying it out to see if he likes it.'

'Seems to be loving it, from where I'm sitting. Totally entranced, when he has this beautiful woman sitting here all alone weeping into her beer with her loneliness.'

'Oh, rubbish, I'm not. I'm possibly just a bit jet-lagged, is all.'

He sighed again. 'It's a crying shame, the way good women are neglected.'

'That's not true,' she retorted. For one thing, who could ever call her a good woman? She wasn't even very useful as a sounding board. She was probably no better than she ought to be, as Auntie Mim would say. And no doubt *had*.

Over at the roulette table Joe caught the croupier's eye and pushed some chips onto the red seventeen. As the wheel started to rotate he threw a glance back at the bar and froze as something like a red hot needle skewered straight through his guts.

He couldn't believe his eyes. That American guy was hanging around Mirandi again, smooching up to her with his smooth looks and phony charm.

Was the guy a fool? His persistence was astounding.

Though he had to admit she was irresistible in that dress. Any man seeing her adorning that bar stool with her rich glossy hair and graceful curves, one long leg swinging a little, would desire her. He'd already warned the guy off once. What more would it take?

It flashed through his mind that it had probably been a mistake to leave her alone.

Although she wasn't a child. She could look after herself. And there was no way she would encourage the guy. Surely.

'*Dix-sept rouge*. Red seventeen,' the croupier intoned, dragging Joe's gaze away.

Frowning, he glanced at the table and saw that his small pile of chips had magically enlarged. Looking around, he saw the anonymous strangers at the table staring at him, some with kindness, others envy, in their hungry eyes.

His gaze lit on the young man who'd been there since early on. The boy's glow of success had long since departed. His chips had dwindled to a few, and for an instant Joe glimpsed a desperation in his eyes that brought his father's face before him with such a gut-wrenching immediacy he nearly swayed in his chair.

He shrugged off the image and steeled himself to focus on his task.

'*Nouveau jeu,*' the croupier announced. 'Your bids, *mesdames et messieurs*?'

Making a hasty selection, Joe shoved some chips forward, then edged his chair around so he could get a better view of the bar.

* * *

Mirandi gave her flirtini a desultory swizzle then popped the maraschino cherry into her mouth. It had an unpleasant, chewy texture. A couple approached the bar and Louis made a huge production of making room for them, in the process finding himself forced to shift to the stool next to hers.

Surprise, surprise.

She noticed his cologne. It smelled expensive, like some artfully manufactured designer fragrance. He smiled at her, stroking his designer bristles while he continued his sly inter-rogation about the shortfalls of her alleged lover.

'I guess *Joe* would have made certain you had some fun too. Did he spin you around the dance floor?' He said Joe's name with a sarcastic inflection she didn't warm to.

'Oh, well, he would have, but...' *Listen* to her, lying through her teeth for a man who'd rather play roulette than spend an hour with her. 'I was tired.'

'You don't look tired.'

Much Louis knew. Her nerves had been so ragged all day she felt exhausted. It was only the adrenaline in the room propping her up. And the knots in her stomach.

'Did you hear the orchestra?' Louis said. 'Not bad for a European outfit.'

He fell silent, swirling the remains of his Scotch musingly around his glass. After a while he glanced at her. 'They have the doors open to the gardens now and people are dancing outside on the terrace.' He lowered his lashes, seduction in his dark eyes, then made a suggestive waggle of his eyebrows. 'Under the moon.'

She had to hand it to Louis for nerve, trying to waltz her off under Joe's very nose. She even contemplated the invitation for a moment. Dancing with Big Shoulders in the moonlight, smelling his classy cologne. He was attractive enough, but everything inside her rose up in revolt.

She glanced across at Joe's broad back. Everything seemed to have gone wrong since they arrived in Monte Carlo. If

only she could get him away from this place, think of a way
to retrieve that wonderful feeling that was growing between
them again in Switzerland, she'd do it, whatever it took.

'Listen, Louis,' she said, 'I'm not in the mood for dancing.
If you wouldn't mind, I'd appreciate it if you'd just—'

'Hey now.' He stopped her, shocked at her forthrightness.
'Don't let's be negative. Come on, what are you drinking?' He
tossed off the remains of his drink, set down his glass and slid
it along to the bartender, adding, 'The lady needs another…
what is it? Ah, sure it is. A flirtini.'

He chuckled.

Joe watched the croupier push the pile of chips towards him
with a curious sense of impatience. Hundreds, five hundreds,
thousands, who cared? Couldn't they hurry it along? He wasn't
a possessive guy by any means, but it gnawed at him that after
the trip and everything they'd said and hadn't said but had
surely meant, not least the night in Zurich, Mirandi would
flirt with some guy.

Here he was putting himself through this harrowing ordeal
and she was fairly tearing a hole in his chest.

He angled around for another glimpse of her and did a
double take. The American had insinuated himself onto the
barstool next to her. His body language said it all. And if Joe
wasn't mistaken, that drink she was holding was *fresh*.

He sprang to his feet and covered the distance between the
roulette table and the bar in less than a click of his fingers. He
bore down on Mirandi Summers, a complex mix of outrage,
disappointment and pure molten rage boiling in his veins, and
snatched the glass from her fingers.

'Joe.' Her startled gaze widened. 'What…?'

He turned on the American guy and snarled, 'Here. Take
this with you.' He stuffed the glass into the guy's hand.

Perhaps dreaming of defending himself, the American

set the glass on the bar. 'Now hang on there, buddy. This lady is—'

'She's with *me*,' Joe informed him through gritted teeth.

The American looked about him as if begging Security to come beefing down on them from all directions, then stood up and held up his hands.

'All right, all right, tough guy. Chill.' He made a mock apologetic gesture to Mirandi. 'Sorry, ma'am, if my presence *offended* you.' Then his amused gaze shifted back to Joe. 'Take it easy, man. No offence intended. Mirandi—I mean *your ladyfriend* here—was looking a little blue. I was only cheering her up.'

He grimaced in what was intended as a suave smile, then swivelled on his heel and made as dignified an exit as a guy could, under those circumstances.

His hackles still bristling, Joe swung around to Mirandi and encountered sparkling emerald anger.

'Just where do you think you are?' she snapped in a low voice. 'That could have been the most ghastly and embarrassing scene. Lucky *Louis* is a gentleman.' She collected her purse and slid off her bar stool.

'*Louis* is a gigolo.'

'Oh, what would you know?' she retorted. 'You were too interested in watching some stupid little spinning ball. For all you cared I could have been getting it on with the bartender.'

'Is he your type?' He felt her withering look but it glanced off him like an arrow. Ridiculously, his emotions seemed to be engaged and he said, far too harshly for the size of the offence, 'I don't know how you could even *think* of encouraging that guy.'

As soon as the words were out he wanted to bite them back, but her expression told him it was too late. She started stalking towards the exit, something it wouldn't have been unpleasant to watch in other circumstances with the voluptuous sway of her hips. He wanted to run after her, but was distracted when an attendant in a tuxedo approached and held out a cloth bag.

'Your winnings, *monsieur*. Please exchange them at the bank.' He indicated the teller's cage at the end of the room.

'Look,' Joe said, exasperated. 'I haven't got time for that now. You take them.' He looked around for Mirandi but there was no sign of her.

'But *monsieur*...' The man appeared shocked. 'I cannot... We must not... It is not permitted...'

'Sorry, mate,' Joe said, pushing past the guy. 'You deal with it. There's someone I need to catch up with.'

What the hell was she playing at? He couldn't see her anywhere in the room. With a nasty lurch he wondered if she'd gone after that American. She was mad enough to do something crazy like that. He'd noticed several times lately that this new Mirandi Summers had quite a temper when she was aroused.

His eye was caught by a flash of red in the adjoining salon.

He took off in pursuit, threading his way through knots of people, dodging waiters, questions resurfacing in his mind at her having allowed the American to chat her up in his very sight.

Faster than the speed of light a million thoughts jabbed his brain. Had she changed this much? Was this how seriously she took him now? He couldn't suppose she was attracted to the guy, not after last night, but whoever knew with women? One minute they seemed to be happy with a man, the next they were headed off into the wild blue yonder ready to take up with the first new gun that came along.

With a sickening jolt he realised that, to be true to himself, if he couldn't trust her he'd have to pull the plug on her. Sever all connections.

Although, perhaps he was overreacting and it needn't come

to that. Probably what he'd witnessed had been nothing more than a conversation. He should, he really should, give her the benefit of the doubt. He entered the next dazzling chamber only to see the red flash of her dress disappear down a hallway, and gritted his teeth with frustration as people got in his way.

Why wouldn't she wait?

He hurried into the hall and had nearly closed the distance between them only to see that it wasn't Mirandi's red dress he was following but some other woman's. Where the hell *was* she?

He glanced about and experienced such a plunge of anxiety he had to stop to draw a few deep breaths and take stock. For God's sake, Joe Sinclair did *not* run an emotional overdraft. Cool it, man. Take a sophisticated view. Nothing had happened. She hadn't gone off with the guy, had she?

As he strode on to the next salon, in an attempt to be rational he fought with the evil genius that had taken over his brain. Face it, this reaction to a little harmless flirting was out of character. Hypocritical, even. How many times had he done the same thing himself? And when had he ever cared what his girlfriends did on the side? If he found out they were dishonest he simply cut them off, no emotion involved.

He *knew* that, but a part of his brain was standing back in bemusement, watching the rest of him get all churned up. It even occurred to him that perhaps this absurd raw feeling as if his guts had been chopped into little pieces was merely the aftermath of the test he'd set himself tonight.

It had been quite confronting, after all. And it had been a long day. Suddenly the unwonted vision of the shock he'd encountered that afternoon popped back into his head and he felt his blood pressure leap to a higher bracket.

His mind shied away from Amelie Sinclair. He'd think about her later. The one thing he *was* dead set certain about was this. Of all the women he'd ever known in his life Mirandi

Summers was the one, the *only* one, he'd never expected to have to doubt.

She really had some explaining to do. When he got his hands on her...

He searched the place, striding grimly from room to room, scanning for that splash of red, often forced to check his stride to avoid a whirling crowd. He was swept into one salon that was grand indeed, its panelled wall space dominated by an enormous and sensuous painting of three lovely nudes. Beneath the incredible rococo ceilings were giant windows festooned with hundreds of metres of satin.

The magnificence was lost on him. There was only one beauty he wanted to lay eyes on, and she wasn't there. He couldn't see her anywhere.

From somewhere close by he heard a lush-stringed tango playing and felt a surge of hope. Something about the music suggested a live orchestra. He turned from the crowded salon and followed the strains until he found himself back in the atrium. The reception was well under way, almost the entire room given over to couples dancing.

And she was there. With a lightening in his chest he saw her across the room, her face pale and wan, clinging to the wall, looking about her for someone. With a violent pang in his gut he thought, *Who?* The American?

He stifled the feeling, and, desperate to talk with her, *reason* with her, wove a path through the crowd of dancers. He was beside her before she had a chance to notice his approach.

He touched her shoulder. 'What the bloody hell do you think you're *doing*?'

She turned with a start, and he saw her momentary look of relief change as she registered his tone. Had he actually shouted?

She stiffened a little. 'I was looking for the entrance.'

'You were planning to leave? By *yourself*?'

'Why not? I'm free and over twenty-one.' She folded her arms and angled away from him.

He compressed his lips, knowing he'd provoked that haughty reaction by his damned impatience. Hell, he really needed to tone himself down. Trouble was, the noise and activity in the room was not conducive to the quiet heart-to-heart he needed with her.

He glanced about for some peaceful corner to take her and noticed that the doors to the terrace had been opened. 'Look, let's get away from this racket.'

She scanned him with a small appraising frown, hesitating, then accompanied him outside into the balmy Mediterranean night without any more trouble. A few couples were strolling the terrace, and he could hear giggles coming from the extensive gardens. His gaze was drawn down a never-ending vista of ponds and fountains.

It was atmospheric down there, he supposed, with all the fountains playing in the moonlight. Shadowy pathways led off to either side, lit by glimmering lights, and here and there classical statues peeped from among the shrubbery, coyly covering their private parts. Some sweet summery scent like honeysuckle flavoured the air.

If only things were different and he could have established some bottom line with Mirandi, a stroll in the moonlit garden with her would not have been a bad thing. Or mightn't have been. If only she hadn't…

He felt something raw in his chest, but his life's practice had been to ignore pain, and he carried on with his usual aplomb. Trouble was, his voice came out sounding strangely hoarse.

'We really need to talk,' he rasped.

'Yes, I think we do.' Though she was still rather proud and stiff, out here in the night air her voice had a sweet silvery quality, as if she were made of magic. He had that feeling of being a huge hulking angry brute while she was a fragile, elusive creature, but the situation had to be faced.

She still had the power to gut him.

But could he just let it happen? Sure she'd grown up a lot, he could see that now, but a guy needed to make his expectations clear. As always he would be civilised about it and employ subtle tactics, though this was one time he felt the need to let her see just where she'd gone wrong and what she was doing to him.

He cleared his throat. 'Look, I've got to tell you I felt—disappointed about you flirting with that guy.'

She looked indignantly at him. 'I *wasn't* flirting.' She sounded so firm and unequivocal, he had to admit it had the ring of truth.

'I saw how he was looking at you.'

'But did you see how I was looking at *him*?'

Always so sassy. Always quick with an answer, he could give her that. She was clever, so bright. No wonder she'd always kept him interested. He felt a wave of intense regret at how much he'd miss that.

'He bought you that drink,' he accused.

'He ordered it before I could stop him. After I told him to get *lost*.' Her mouth trembled. 'He forced it on me and I just… You're not listening to me, are you? You never listen. You haven't listened to a word I've said all day. You just went ahead and risked your—your *life*…'

His guts were churning. 'Is that why you did it? You were angry. You wanted to punish me?'

'I wasn't angry. I was—*scared*. Anyway…' her voice wobbled, with all the emotion running high '…since when do you care who I talk to?'

'Since always.' The truth of that statement tightened around his chest like a garotte.

He thought of that awful day when she was just a kid and he'd had to tell her it was over.

She was twisting her hands in front of her, her graceful white arms satin in the moonlight. 'Oh, that's just not true,

Joe. You didn't care about me back then, not the littlest bit, even though I told you... I all but *told* you, how I—I... You wanted to live free and easy. That's what you said. You didn't want to clutter your life with responsibilities.'

He closed his eyes. 'I *had* to say that. It couldn't go anywhere with us, could it?' Something had a stranglehold on his larynx and was putting his voice through a strainer. 'Look, it was ten years ago. We both knew you were too young. Your father said... Even *I* could see he was right. You needed to go to uni. How great a life would it have been with no money coming in?'

Her eyes glistened with tears. 'As if it was ever about money. It never even occurred to you that day, did it, that I might be...? What I'd come to tell you. No, of course it didn't,' she muttered. 'You couldn't have known. And even if you had you'd have run twice as fast.' She made a hopeless little gesture. 'Oh, I'm such a fool. I don't know why I agreed to come. I let myself get sucked in all over again in Zurich, and here we are. So over, how could I even have...?' Her voice choked and she turned sharply away from him.

A gentle breeze messed a few strands of her hair and when she lifted her hand to smooth it he could see that her fingers were trembling. He cast about for something to say but his speech was paralysed. Suddenly an almighty black catastrophe was bearing down on him and he felt helpless to avert it.

'This was such a mistake,' she said, her voice nearly as hoarse as his. She turned for the stairs that led down to the garden. 'I'm going home.'

He watched her step down onto the garden walk, the impassioned phrases they'd hurled at each other rolling around in his head in meaningless clusters, his whole being churned up in a way he scarcely recognised.

She was walking quickly away with her head high, but even from behind he could tell she was crying. He stood there like a clumsy thunderstruck oaf while she rounded a bend in the path, then disappeared from his view, hidden by the shrubbery and the walls of a small folly that had been built to resemble some Roman temple.

All at once the cold reality that she was seriously walking away from him for all eternity slammed into him and a bolt of pure panic galvanised him to action.

He bounded down the steps after her and sprinted to catch her up. 'Wait, Mirandi… *Wait*.' She didn't pause, instead her step quickened and he had a suffocating sense of déjà vu, as if he were back in the dream. At least this was real life and his legs could work, and he swiftly covered the ground between them and came up alongside her.

'What couldn't I have known? What? What did you mean?' Panting, urgent, he grabbed her arms and forced her to stand still. 'What would I have run from?'

She trembled in his hands, her arms cool in the night air. In the dim light she was whiter than he'd ever seen, her lovely face strained and streaked with tears. 'Are you sure you want to know? It's something *sad*, Joe.'

He said roughly, his voice as hoarse as a foghorn, 'Don't you think I might have already known sad things once or twice?'

She lowered her wet lashes. 'Oh, I know. You have, of course.' She moistened her lips. 'All right, then.' She glanced around, making sure no one was nearby to overhear. Then she said in a low voice, 'What I meant to tell you that day, and would have if you'd been more welcoming, was that I was—expecting.'

He felt the blood drain from his heart. *'What?'*

She nodded. 'I'd only just found out.' She broke away from him and made a helpless gesture. 'I was in such a spin I didn't know *what* to do. I thought if I told you, but—well, you know how things went.'

He reeled away from her, flooded by the most appalling guilt and remorse. 'Oh. Oh, my God.' He clutched his forehead, ran his hand through his hair while his wits tried to assemble the facts.

A pregnant girl came to see him, to inform she was with child, *his* child, and he was intent on rejecting her. For her own good.

'Oh, no,' he ground out. 'My poor girl. Mirandi, I—I don't know what to say. I'm so very sorry. If only I'd known. I—I wish I hadn't had to…' He closed his eyes. 'I wish it hadn't been like that.' A jolting thought struck him. 'So where is your—your child?'

His child.

'There isn't one,' she said baldly, dashing sudden tears away with the back of her hand. 'I only managed to keep him inside a couple of months and…something went wrong, I guess. I lost him.'

His guts clenched as though held in a vice. He imagined her rounded and vulnerable, and a groan escaped him as the implications of what she must have gone through lacerated his guilty conscience.

He *had* to ask, though he hardly dared for fear of what her answer might be. 'Sweetheart, did you—did your father *know* you were pregnant that day you came to see me?'

She shook her head and he could feel that measure of relief, at least. At least the captain hadn't begged him to cut his daughter loose knowing she was with child.

With a womanly dignity that impressed him, he saw her make a visible effort to control her emotions.

She said in a low voice, 'I was in Brisbane when it happened. When I—when I lost the baby. That was why I *chose* Brisbane, so I could put some distance between my family and—everyone before I broke the news. I was scared of telling Dad. As it turned out, I never needed to. It was—quite a—a painful time.' Her voice croaked on the word and he felt his heartstrings twist savagely.

'Oh, sweetheart.' He put his arms around her, drew her

against his chest and laid his cheek against her hair. He could feel her soft breasts, her heart beating against his own. He pressed her to him and stroked her, struggling with the old dilemma. Tell her the whole truth and risk turning her against her dad? Hurt her even more?

She angled her face into his neck and even in the exigency of emotion the scent of her rose in his nostrils like an aphrodisiac.

'I should've been there,' he said painfully. 'I should've been *with* you…'

'Oh, Joe.' She sighed and her breath fanned his neck. 'What would have been the use? You were already tired of me. You're tired of me now.'

'I wasn't tired of you. I'm not—I could *never* be tired of you.' He felt some hard inner shell give inside his chest and suddenly he was awash with raw, hot emotion and truth could no longer be contained. 'It *killed* me to break it off,' he said, his voice as rough as if it were being strained through gravel. 'Afterwards I missed you… All those nights I *ached* for you… A hundred times I nearly gave in and texted you.'

'Then why…?

'Because I knew he was right, your father. It didn't matter how angry I felt, how—rebellious, I s'pose—I knew it was true. You were too young and I had nothing to give you. I wasn't even sure of what direction I wanted to go in. I'm *still* not sure.'

'Oh, Joe, Dad doesn't think like that.'

He held her a little away from him and ruefully scanned her face. How well did she understand her father?

Moisture glistened on her lashes. Her sensuous mouth was so soft and luscious his blood quickened with desire, and whatever else he *should* have said the time for talking was over. Unable to resist, with a groan he took her sweet lips, tenderly at first, then as her soft curves sank against him and he had the taste of her, God help him, he was overtaken with lust and kissed her deeply and hungrily.

The sound of approaching voices made an annoying distraction. But he was as hard as a log, and, trembling with urgency, he drew her off the path and into a shadowy niche between some dense, fragrant shrubs and the stone balustrade of the folly.

As he hid with her there in the secluded shadowy place, all at once the moonlit night seemed to ping with a taut expectation, as if reckless spirits were winging on the vibrant air. Bending to taste her white satin throat, he heard her quickened breath, felt her breasts rise and fall under his hands, and his passion to have her intensified.

For an instant he paused, and it was like the lull before the storm. He sensed her answering excitement as she panted in his arms, aroused by their forbidden location, infected by the honeysuckle-scented magic of the night.

The electric moment intensified, then he took her mouth, kissing her back against the wall while he unzipped his trousers and allowed his straining shaft its grateful freedom. Her fragrance, part perfumed sweetness, part primitive, aroused woman, stormed his senses in an irresistible erotic invasion. With lustful haste he dragged up the red dress. Already her undies were excitingly moist, and he tore them away with hands that shook, inflamed by the exposure of the delicious curls. Positioning her carefully, he supported her bottom with his hands while she clung to his neck and wrapped her legs around his waist, then he thrust into her, evoking a guttural cry from deep in her throat.

He drove and drove again, deeper and harder, while she gripped him with her thighs and met him thrust for thrust, her hot, slick walls blissfully tight around his length. The sweet, painful pressure mounted, but he held himself back from the ultimate ecstasy until he felt her first honeyed spasm grip him like a heavenly vice, then his orgasm broke in a hot, wild release of rushing seed.

As her last rapturous cries melted into silence he held her panting in his arms, tasting the sweet, slightly salt sweat on her neck.

She was *his*, was all he was capable of thinking. He couldn't let her go again. He couldn't.

CHAPTER TWELVE

SOMETHING crept into Mirandi's awareness, strange bird calls, followed some time later by occasional muffled bumps and thuds. Then much later sudden flurries of voices, surprisingly close, and sounds of gushing water that might have come from outside.

Sensing the morning, she swam closer to consciousness. She had an awareness then of a feeling of warmth down the length of her back, a solid, comfortable presence she'd relied on through the night.

She opened her eyes. As she blinked at the light issuing through chinks in the curtains she had the sensation the morning was well advanced. Gradually the mists of sleep dispersed and everything came crowding back.

The casino and her quarrel with Joe. She'd come so close to throwing in the towel again, but somehow the situation had turned about and… Had that *really* happened? Love in the casino gardens, just like their wild old days? She smiled, remembering it all with that intoxicated, laughing, rapturous walk home.

As she turned Joe's words over in her mind about their ancient break-up she almost felt like pinching herself. After all the anguish she'd suffered back then, to discover that he'd broken her heart with the best of intentions evoked some mixed feelings. Had he somehow found out about her family's concerns? She must have let it leak out. She wrinkled her brow in the effort to recall. It was all so long ago the sequence of events had blurred in her mind, except of course for her secret grief. She had no doubt that would stay with her for ever, sharp and clear.

But she was so glad she'd told him the truth at last. It was as though her confession had unlocked a door between them. There were still questions she needed to ask, though. Perhaps, when the time was ripe...

The time. Oh, damn. The conference. Her pleasant glow doused, she lifted her head to squint at the bedside clock and saw it had already reached ten-thirty. Too late, surely, though if they hurried up she supposed they could make the middle sessions.

If only Joe weren't such a stickler for work.

Easing around, she saw that he was still deeply asleep. Gingerly she lifted his protective arm from across her body and slid out of the bed. He barely stirred.

She hesitated a moment, then gently replaced the covers over him. In sleep the deep lines around his eyes and mouth had smoothed, and he looked younger, less careworn. This must have been his first real sleep since they left Sydney. Waking him would be such a pity.

She tiptoed to the bathroom. With hunger gnawing at her insides she spent no more than twenty minutes in the shower, restraining a bubbling desire to warble at the top of her voice, then, when she'd dried herself in the big fluffy Metropole towel, she wrapped the robe around her and padded out to rummage through her suitcase for something to wear.

'Come here.'

Startled, she looked around and saw Joe leaning up on his elbow, his jaw dark with stubble, a seductive smile playing on his sensuous lips. With a laugh she sashayed across the room, then dived into his bristly embrace.

'Do you know what the time is?' she panted when she was finally free to breathe, tracing the line of his gorgeous bones from cheekbone to roughened jaw with one delicate fingertip. 'As your MA, I think I should warn you that you've missed two conference sessions already.'

His brows edged together as he examined her with a gleaming gaze. 'I think you're taking this MA role too seriously. Haven't you heard that the Côte d'Azur should be a place to relax?'

'Yeah,' she said in a dispirited tone, rolling her eyes. 'I've *heard* it. If only I could try it.'

He grinned. 'How about we hire one of those spots under the beach umbrellas and find out how swimming in the Mediterranean compares with Coogee?'

She bounded upright and squealed. 'Oh, *yes*. Now you're talking.'

'And since we're here, we might as well have a look around and see what other fleshpots we can plunge into. But first...' He planted a light kiss on her swollen lips, then cast the covers aside and rose magnificently from the bed. 'I could eat a lion.'

A pavement café with a view of the marina served them a delicious brunch of omelettes and crusty rolls with a Provençal salad and coffee. Joe's tension of the day before seemed to have eased. It was as if he'd walked through some trial of fire and come safely out on the other side. Today he'd reverted to his easy-going self, though there were moments of silence between them when Mirandi still sensed areas of reserve.

She did some thinking of her own. Last night had certainly indicated that Joe's passion for her continued unabated, but her dream of an ongoing relationship felt a little shaky. Desire didn't necessarily mean love, and love as she understood it meant trust and unconditional honesty.

Though which came first? And how could she demand the one without first being secure in the other? Maybe she was wanting too much. Maybe souls were all entitled to their secrets and she should just be patient and wait for the cards to fall as they would.

She relaxed in her chair under the awning and spread strawberry jam on her roll, enjoying the ocean breeze whispering through her hair.

'Feeling good today?' she ventured.

Joe smiled. 'Much better.' He reached out and took her hand. 'Thanks to you. If you hadn't been with me last night...'

'*Moi?* But you were so angry with me.'

He looked rueful. 'Yeah, I know. I was—I have to admit—a bit jealous. Does that shock you?'

'I don't know. I'd have been jealous of *you* if I'd thought you were chatting up a blonde. As it was, I was jealous of the roulette wheel.'

He smiled. 'No need to be ever again. That was my first and last dance with the spinning witch.'

'Truly?' She looked keenly at him.

'Truly. I find I don't have an aptitude for it.'

She felt such a flood of relief. 'Oh, Joe. That's *such* good news.' After a moment she sent him another sidelong glance. 'Is that why you needed to do it? To find out?'

He nodded. 'Yeah. Funny how I'd built it up in my mind. I guess I was afraid I might get hooked like my old man. It's good to know I can take it or leave it like any ordinary Joe.'

She smiled behind her sunglasses. As if he would ever be ordinary. Not to her, at any rate.

Swimming seemed risky after such a feast, so they bought hats at a boutique, donned their cameras and joined the tourists strolling around the town, delighted by the maze of narrow paved alleyways and sunny courtyards, the overhead balconies dripping with geranium or bougainvillea.

In the shopping boulevards every luxury brand imaginable seemed represented behind the discreet awnings, and classic car shops abounded. After Joe had needed to pause for a close examination of at least his seventh expensive Italian auto parked in the street, Mirandi was grateful for his suggestion that they cool off in the sea.

The Metropole boasted its own private beach just a two minute ride away. By Australian standards it was cramped, with every available centimetre packed with sun worshippers on their hired loungers, but swimming in the sea was as exhilarating as ever.

'This is peaceful, isn't it?' Joe said, lazing beside her under the umbrella, drops of sea water glistening among the black whorls of hair on his bronzed chest. 'You know, I can't remember having a holiday since I was a kid.' He turned his smiling blue gaze to hers. 'How would it feel to stay on a few extra days? Maybe find a place further along the coast, perhaps at Cap Ferrat or Villefranche?'

'Oh, *Joe*, I'd love that.' She beamed at him until reality intruded and her smile faltered a bit. 'Can we do that, though? What about work?'

'I'm sure I can arrange it. CEOs do get to have some time off. I'll make an executive decision. How about it?' He smiled and she could see the tiny lines crinkle at the corners of his eyes under his dark glasses.

She grinned back. 'Do you really need to ask?' After a second she added cautiously, 'But, er…how will you explain me staying on with you?'

'Ah, yes.' His brows edged together. 'That might require some ingenuity. We may have to make it a study tour of Provence, like politicians do.'

She laughed. 'Why not a study tour of Europe? Then we could stay a year.'

Later that afternoon, lounging back in her spa tub at the Metropole among the bubbles and the floating rose petals, she said dreamily, 'And there were you, dreading coming to Provence. You seem to have taken to it very well.'

There was a fine line of beading along Joe's upper lip. 'Well, I am half French.'

Her nerves jumped, though she tried to be nonchalant. 'You've never really mentioned that.'

'Haven't I? No. No, *well…*' He rested his head against the side of the tub and closed his eyes. She felt his hand tighten on her leg.

She waited, then after a while said, 'That was your mother in the lobby, wasn't it?'

He let out a breath. 'I guess.'

'You—haven't seen her for a while?'

'Since I was fourteen.'

'She seemed quite devastated to see you.'

'Did she?'

After quite a long time, when she thought he wouldn't say any more, he said, 'I scarcely know her.'

'Aren't you curious?'

'About what?'

'How she—*who* she is.'

'I can guess,' he growled.

It felt prudent not to pursue the delicate topic any further, and Mirandi gave herself up to days of hedonistic pleasure. Dancing in nightclubs, swimming, though sometimes on the beach she thought of those long, soft, sandy crescents she'd taken for granted at home. They dined every evening on delicious fare prepared by some of the world's finest chefs, then later, were lucky to find a villa to rent on the outskirts of the tiny village of Sancerre-sur-Mer with a rocky path from their garden down to a tiny beach, and settled in for a week of idyllic relaxation.

Joe hired a car and drove them far and wide, to explore hillside villages perched incredibly on the edges of cliffs, with narrow, twisting mediaeval streets. He seemed keen to get in touch with his French side, and visited every little museum and bookshop in the area to delve for local history. They hired bicycles, and on a hot, hot day rode along a hill path, swam in the chill waters of a stream, and in the shade of a dense grove of trees picnicked on cheese, fresh crusty bread from the local *boulangerie*, and a delicious flaky pissaladière tart filled with anchovy and olives washed down with white wine.

'I'll be so fat,' Mirandi said, stretching out on a patch of grass to stare at the cerulean sky. 'All this lovely food.'

'All the better.' Joe was sprawled out with his head cushioned on the canvas picnic-pack. 'I'd love to see you all plump and cuddly.'

'You say that *now*.' She rolled over on her tummy and plucked a blade of grass, then tickled him under his chin with it. 'Aren't you going to see her before we leave?'

He closed his eyes and didn't answer for an age. She began to wonder if he'd even heard her question, then he opened his lids and pierced her with a glinting blue glance.

'It's not as simple as that.'

'Why not? Do you know where she lives?'

'She has a villa in Antibes,' he conceded reluctantly. 'At least she—*had* one. She lives there with her husband. Or for all I know she could be onto her third, fourth or fifth husband.'

'Oh. What makes you think she's had so many husbands?'

'I don't *know* she has. I'm guessing.' She looked queryingly at him and he let out an exasperated breath. 'Oh, all right. Perhaps she hasn't. She walked out on us when I was nine, or thereabouts.'

'Why did she leave?'

He made a grimace. 'Oh, probably over the gambling. The disease really had him by then.'

'Didn't she want to take you with her?'

He evaded her eyes. When he spoke his voice was so deep and gruff she needed to strain her ears to hear him properly. 'She tried. She moved into a flat over in Ryde, packed up all my clothes, and transported it all there in a taxi. But I—wouldn't stay. I ran away and caught the train home.'

'Oh. Didn't you get on with her?'

He was silent again. Then as if the words were torn from deep inside him he growled, 'I did, in fact. I—loved her. But I couldn't leave Dad.'

'Oh.' The poignant simplicity of the story moved her, and she had to turn her face away so he wouldn't see the tears blurring her eyes. 'Didn't she come to visit you?'

His pain almost tangible, he put his arm over his eyes. 'Yes, she did, often enough, but she'd never stay. Dad—*I*—wanted her to. It was too painful after a while for Dad. She kept begging me to go with her and I got angry one day. I said things, as kids do. She must have given up hope then, I s'pose, because she left Sydney and came back here to her family.' After a small charged silence he said, 'She used to write to me.'

'Did you write back?'

After an eternity he said, 'No. I…well, I never opened the letters.'

'Oh.' She sighed. 'That's such a shame.'

He removed his arm and lifted his head to look at her. 'Well, it would have felt like a betrayal of Dad. You see?'

She shrugged. 'I guess.' A deep silence fell, and in the stillness she could hear insects whirring in some nearby gorse. Every so often the faint breeze carried the scent of lavender from a nearby farm. Joe sank back, his eyes closed.

She said, pursuing the delicate thread, 'But you did come over here at some point. You mentioned being here for that weekend.'

He glanced across at her, curling a corner of his lip. 'Oh, yes. It was after the funeral. She came to Sydney for it and insisted I come back here with her. I was only fourteen and—in a bit of a—black hole, so to speak, after…so I… Well, I was pleased to have somewhere to *go*. And I—liked her. I trusted her, but of course when we arrived here I discovered she had a new man.'

'Oh, Joe.' Her heart welled with pity and she couldn't prevent a rush of tears. She crawled over and lay on top of him with her arms around him. She could feel his big heart thumping against hers through their thin cotton clothes as he held her tight, tolerating her teary kisses.

'Sorry, sorry,' she said after a while, mopping up after Joe was forced to comfort *her*. 'So what happened when you were here?'

'He probably wasn't even such a bad bloke, but you know, I was a boy, and I couldn't live with it. Anyway, after a pretty bleak weekend, I forced them to pay my way back. I'm sure her partner was only too glad to put me on the plane. Then in Sydney I moved in with my cousin Neil until the law said I was old enough to fend for myself. You must remember Neil.' She nodded, and he smiled grimly. 'Yeah. Neil was twenty-one at the time and a bit of a wild lad himself, though you'd never know it now.' His smile warmed in recollection of his wild beginnings. 'I'll always be grateful to Neil.' He shrugged and spread his hands. 'Anyway, the rest is history.'

'But it's not over yet.'

'Isn't it?' He turned lazily to look at her, though his eyes were alert. 'What does that mean, Miss Summers?'

'Well…' She gazed into his eyes. 'You're here. You're an adult now. You can see it all through a man's eyes. I'm sure *she*…your mother…'

'Amelie.'

'Amelie? Oh, that's such a lovely name. Well, I'm sure she'd be open to—talking to you at least.'

'I doubt it. No, no way.' He shook his head with conviction. 'Not after all the times I…rejected her. Anyway, there's no point. What would be the point?'

'The *point*.' She sat up and brushed herself down. 'Well, she's your mother. In my view that's a pretty strong point. Having grown up without one, even though I had Auntie Mim and I love the dear old girl despite everything, if I had the chance—just *one* chance to spend an hour with my mother before I die…' Her voice wobbled. 'Even five minutes. *One* minute. I'd fly across the world. I'd shift heaven and earth for that minute.'

He gazed quizzically at her for a moment, then his black lashes screened his eyes. After a minute or two he hauled himself up with his usual athletic grace and stood, stretching out his hand to her. 'Come. Siesta will be over now in the town. Didn't you say you wanted to do some shopping for dinner?'

Joe didn't speak of his mother again that evening, although Mirandi ventured one further question over their ravioli and salad.

'What became of her letters?'

He looked curiously at her. 'Amelie's?' His eyes slid away from her, and he gave an off-hand shrug. 'Oh, they're somewhere, I suppose.'

Somewhere. Then not destroyed. Not torn to shreds or burned to ashes in some backyard bonfire. That suggested they were kept by someone. Someone who cared deep down, perhaps. At least these were Mirandi's musings, though she was careful not to reveal them.

The following day was their last before the precious time ended and they flew back to reality. It started early with a swim before breakfast. The sea was too chilly at that hour for Mirandi to stay long, so she waved to Joe and climbed the rocky steps up to their villa with chattering teeth.

Half an hour later, with coffee brewing, she set orange juice, yoghurt, strawberries and wild raspberries on the terrace table, and waited for Joe to arrive with the basket of warm croissants from the boulangerie.

It wasn't long before they were facing each other over breakfast.

'I was wondering,' Joe said, about to bite into a croissant with his white teeth, 'if you would care to drive into Antibes today?'

Mirandi's ears pricked up, but she concealed her surge of

interest. Silly to leap to conclusions. A drive might be no more than that. She said as calmly as she could, 'I'd love to. Any particular reason?'

'Possibly.' He lifted his shoulders, gruffness in his voice. 'We'll see.'

Since Joe wasn't sure any more of his mother's surname, he used the Internet to search for her telephone number. The last surname he had for her was Bonnard. If a Bonnard still lived at the old address, he would have to assume it was still hers and her husband's. As it turned out, the initial to the Christian name was all that had changed in the directory listing. Now, it seemed, there was only an A. Bonnard.

Finding her number was the easy part. Dialling it was something else. Mirandi left him to make the call in privacy, though she was agog to know the outcome.

'She'll see us at noon,' Joe said, emerging from the bedroom. Though his voice was steady, she sensed a tension in him that hadn't been there for days.

'How did she sound?'

'I don't know.' His voice sounded strained. 'She—she didn't take the call. It was Marie I spoke to. The housekeeper.'

Mirandi crossed her fingers. Oh, for a successful visit.

The drive to Antibes was spectacular, though Joe didn't have too much to say, possibly because he was concentrating on the road. Just possibly. Or perhaps he was feeling as nerve-racked as Mirandi.

They followed the Corniche as far as Nice, and enjoyed breathtaking views of sea and coast, as well as some hair-raising bends. Antibes wasn't a great deal further on from Nice and the hire car's navigation guide helped them find the correct address.

When they drew up at the villa with ivy trailing over the pink stone walls and twining itself around high black ironwork gates, Joe turned off the ignition and sat in silence, his hands clenching the wheel.

Mirandi noticed the tiny pulse throbbing at his temple. 'I'll wait here,' she said after several minutes.

He gave a small start and turned to her. 'Are you sure?'

She smiled and touched his hand. 'It's your meeting.'

He leaned over to kiss her, then got out of the car and straightened his jeans and jacket. In the side vision mirror she watched him brace himself, run a finger around the inside of his shirt collar, then stride up to the gate and ring the bell.

Almost at once the gates opened.

CHAPTER THIRTEEN

Joe walked up the path and climbed the few steps to the small stone portico, conscious of his increased heartrate and moistening palms. The heavy front door was ajar, the same maid standing there in wait as had stood on his previous arrival, albeit with twenty more years of living lining her grave face, and touches of silver at her temples.

'*Bonjour*, Marie,' he said. 'Do you remember me?'

'Of course, M. Joe,' she said, bowing her head. '*Mais bienvenue. Madame* expects you. Please…'

He followed her along a hall, then through some glass doors and across a small walled courtyard cooled partly by an orange tree and partly by Aphrodite, who was rising from the centre of a fountain and projecting a graceful spray through her eternally pursed lips.

He remembered it all with a curious tug in his chest, though it seemed smaller than he'd thought, apart from the tree, which could have done with a prune. Marie led him across the courtyard and into another part of the house. She knocked on a door, then showed him into a long, light room with a glass ceiling at one end.

A strong aroma of paint and turpentine assailed him, and one part of his brain registered numerous canvases stacked against the walls.

His mother was standing by a sturdy work table, wiping her hands with a cloth. She continued to wipe as he approached her, and he saw with a shock that her hands were trembling. Then he realised that all of her diminutive frame was atremble.

He felt such a rush of emotion that for a moment he couldn't speak. He noticed that her soft eyes were moist, or it might have been his own.

'*Bonjour, Maman*,' he said hoarsely. 'I am sorry... So sorry...'

'Oh,' she said, dropping the cloth and holding out her hands. '*Joey*. Here you are.'

Mirandi waited and listened to music for nearly an hour, then got out of the car and strolled up and down the street. After several turns, she heard someone calling and saw a woman beckoning her from Joe's mother's gate.

Smiling uncertainly, she walked back. The woman introduced herself as Marie. '*Madame* would like you to visit with us, if you please, *mam'selle*.'

She beamed. 'That would be lovely, Marie. Thank you.'

Marie showed her through the villa to a small sheltered loggia with two open sides giving magnificent views of the Mediterranean. Joe and his mother were seated at a table charmingly set with three places.

Joe rose when Mirandi stepped out onto the flagged floor of the balcony, and swiftly took her hand. '*Maman*, this is Mirandi. Mirandi, may I present Mme Bonnard.'

Joe's mother greeted her warmly and invited her to sit. Throughout the lunch she listened with great attention to everything Mirandi said, though her eyes rested fondly on her son's face more often than not. Joe laughed often, and Mirandi couldn't help but be aware that sometimes both his and his mother's eyes seemed to acquire a moist shimmer.

There was much unspoken emotion in the air, though Amelie still managed to insert some penetrating questions into the conversation vis-à-vis Mirandi's work, her living arrangements in Sydney and her family history, dating back before the invasion.

In some ways the gentle interrogation was so typical of

Mim's whenever Mirandi had taken a friend home for tea, Mirandi felt quite comfortable with it.

There were several points in the conversation when Amelie's gentle glance shifted from Joe to Mirandi and back, and Mirandi knew there was no doubt in the Frenchwoman's mind of her passion for Joe.

After the lunch, Amelie began to wilt a little, and Mirandi remembered siesta was the custom in Provence. Comprehending at the same time, Joe exchanged a glance with Mirandi and they took their leave, each of them shaking hands with Amelie and being kissed on both cheeks.

There was more kissing at the front door, and Amelie held both of Joe's hands and said, 'Come again, my son. Please.'

The plea was heartfelt, and Mirandi understood it was a wrench for them both to part after having found each other again for such a brief time. Perhaps that was why Joe was nearly as silent on the journey back to Sancerre-sur-Mer as he'd been on the journey to Antibes, though this time his silence had a different quality. Often Mirandi felt his gaze drift her way as though she was in his thoughts, and once or twice his hand strayed to touch her.

That evening when she was packing her suitcase and arranging what she needed to wear on the plane, he came into the room with a pensive frown.

'Ah...I've been thinking.' He dragged a hand through his hair. 'You know...one visit with my mother in twenty years doesn't seem very fair to her, does it? Who knows when I'll have the time to come back here?' He shot her a glance, drifted across to the window and gazed out.

'I know,' she said warmly. 'It was so wonderful meeting her. It's a pity we don't have more time.'

'It *is*. Yes, it is,' he agreed with enthusiasm. 'That's why I've been thinking... At least one of us will have to go back or the firm will think we've absconded.' He gave a small laugh.

He turned to face her, his face filled with a light she hadn't seen before, then advanced and took her shoulders in his hands. For some reason her heart started to sink. 'Sweetheart, how confident do you feel about flying back to Sydney on your own?'

'Oh.' Her heart took a definite plunge, but she knew when it was time to put on a bright face. 'I'm fine with it. Course I am. Hey, an intrepid traveller like me?' She grinned to demonstrate her complete lack of concern. 'Why, how—long do you think you might stay?'

'Probably not long. A few days, a week? Two? Just long enough—so I can get to know her again. Do you understand?'

'Of course I do, Joe. It's a wonderful idea, and very important.'

'I knew you'd understand.' He looked suddenly twitchy, as if he was somehow all up in the air. 'Are you sure you don't mind? You won't be nervous on your own?'

'Nervous? *Moi*?'

Terrified more like, because she could see where this was heading. His newly discovered French side was taking over and he would never come home.

'Don't you worry about me,' she lied with phony bravado. 'I have nerves of steel. I'm a market analyst now, remember?'

'Yes, yes, of course,' he said heartily. 'And don't you worry. When you go to work next Monday morning Patterson will show you to your new office.'

'Will he?' Suddenly she felt almost faint. Everything was already arranged. He'd been on the phone to Patterson, spoken to people at work. The reality of work was looming and she'd have to face it without Joe.

She might have to face everything without Joe. Life. The future.

It was an emotional farewell at the airport in Nice, on her side at any rate. Joe kept putting his arms around her and kissing her, and she had to fight to hold herself together. What if she never saw him again? Stranger things had happened.

When he kissed her goodbye for the last time, she said, 'You will come home, won't you?'

'You'd better believe it.'

And he laughed. But it was a happy laugh. Not the laugh of a man contemplating a separation from the woman he loved. Whereas she… All she could think of was how would she be without him now? How would she *sleep*?

It could very well mean she *wasn't* the woman he loved.

On the plane she tried to console herself with the reflection that Joe had conquered some demons on this trip and would be much the happier for it. *Happier but in France*, her evil genius chipped in.

She was surprised when she finally landed at Sydney airport to see Ryan Patterson waiting for her. Patterson, of all people. Joe had organised it from France, Patterson told her. To ease her back into her job.

If that wasn't a sign she didn't know what was. If ever there was a man Joe had shown no confidence in whatsoever, Patterson was the man. And now she'd been handed over to him.

It was the old story. There was a new woman in Joe's life, and it wasn't Mirandi Summers.

She visited Mim and her father and told them she'd been to Provence with Joe. They both looked startled over the sponge cake and teacups to hear of Joe's successes, and Mim exclaimed, 'Joe *Sinclair*? Who'd ever believe he'd amount to anything?'

Her father lifted his brows at Mim. 'Joe? No, no, you've got him wrong, Mim. Joe was a bright lad, and good-hearted underneath. He knew how to keep his word.'

Mirandi's ears pricked up. 'What do you mean by that, Dad?'

Her father sent his sister a look and Mim frowned and gave

her head a very slight shake. Not so slight that Mirandi missed it, though.

Her curiosity piqued, she looked from one to the other evasive face. 'What?' she prompted. 'What is it?'

Her father's eyes met Mirandi's then slid away. 'Well…'

Mirandi's heart started to beat really fast. 'Is this…is this something about Joe and me, Dad? Something I don't know about?'

Embarrassed, her father looked down at his teacup. 'Well, it was only ever intended for the best for both of you. Joe needed to establish himself. He had no one else…'

'He had me,' she said quietly, her pulse suddenly booming in her ears.

Her father lifted his rueful gaze to hers. 'You were too young, love, to take on that job. I'm sorry you—went through a bad time, but I acted for the best. I couldn't have—we could never have guessed how hard you'd take it.' On the edge of her vision Mirandi noticed Mim dab at her eyes, while the captain went on, 'We thought…we honestly thought you'd get over it in a few weeks at most, once you started at uni.'

Mirandi could feel herself turning white, but she held herself together. 'What did you do? You went to see Joe? You said things to him?'

Her father sighed. His bluff face was so kind, so wise, and sometimes so *wrong*.

'It wasn't like that. I just—pointed out to him how *young* you were. He—saw the force of my argument. And I was right, you know. Look how well you've done. You've *both* done.'

'You hurt him, Dad,' she said hoarsely. 'You hurt him.'

Mim started to weep quietly and Mirandi rose abruptly to her feet. 'I'll have to think about this.'

'But you've found each other again, haven't you?' Mim cried after her when Mirandi was rushing out the front door. 'Isn't that what you came to tell us?'

'I don't *know*,' Mirandi said.

CHAPTER FOURTEEN

HER emotions ran high for days, but when Mirandi had digested the shock she eventually stopped agonising. It was of no use to blame them. At least she understood now so many of those oblique things Joe had said to her. Her father had done it out of love, and who was to know how things would have turned out otherwise? Joe might have dumped her soon enough anyway.

She let them invite her around for Sunday dinner and showed them some of her photos. At least now she was in charge of her life, and she could choose to be with Joe and no one could prevent her. Except for Joe himself, of course. She couldn't repress a pang of fear at the thought.

She had other reasons to be emotional. For one, she was yearning for Joe night and day. She knew she was probably being irrational, but her imagination had been going berserk since that last goodbye. Sometimes at night when she was sprinkling her pillow with tears, she told herself that, after all they'd been through together, in the end the love of her life had relegated her back to being a mere employee.

Her new job could probably be quite interesting once she started concentrating on it properly. Somehow though, without Joe, even the new office had lost its relish. The meetings weren't nearly as intriguing knowing that Joe wasn't lurking about threatening to stride by looking autocratic and dripping with hotness.

As well, a couple of her colleagues who'd thought she was a lowly assistant were quite snotty when they discovered she was a bona fide MA with her own office. At least Ryan was supportive. She thanked him for it one day and he said cheerfully, 'Boss's orders. I've been instructed to look after you.'

What? He'd been *instructed* to be her friend?

She could have burst into tears on the spot. She'd never felt so alone. Though, forcing herself to look on the bright side, she probably could have picked herself up and sashayed around the office like a goddess if only she hadn't always felt so deathly tired. In fact, it wasn't impossible she was coming down with dengue fever. Who knew what a woman could catch in the Mediterranean?

Joe emailed her often, but it wasn't the same. Anything could be said in an email. It wasn't like looking into the person's eyes. To prove her point she emailed back with bright snappy chatter about how fantastic everything was. How absolutely *fine* she felt. How bursting with ideas she was for running the company.

Joe's week had stretched into three the day the bombshell dropped. She was standing in her office reading through some policy files when Ryan Patterson dropped in and told her that Joe had resigned from the firm.

She simply froze. The blow was so extreme she felt unable to speak, just forced a shattered smile for Patterson, then as soon as he left the room she had to rush to the bathroom to throw up.

How could Joe not have told her? He'd emailed her only the day before. To *resign*. Just like that, without warning. Her worst, most maniacal fears were realised to the fullest extent. Provence had crept into his heart and he couldn't tear himself away.

For the rest of the week, bereft of her lover, her faith in humanity destroyed, she walked through the days like an automaton. An automaton that needed to throw up every morning, that was.

On Saturday, grateful for the reprieve from having to put on a cheery office face to confound those witches on the fourteenth floor, she stayed in bed. There was something in the bathroom she didn't want to see.

At least the girls she shared with were away for the weekend, thank goodness. It didn't matter how blotchy and miserable she looked, so she gave herself up to an emotional binge and let the floodgates open wide. Fifty billion megalitres of water exploded over the floodway.

This was why, when the security intercom buzzed, she ignored it. It repeated several times, and then whoever it must have been was either let in by other tenants or had given up and left. Not that she cared. They wouldn't be buzzing for her. No one would ever buzz for her again.

She was dragged from her soggy tissues by the sound of someone brisk hammering on the door of the flat. Someone with a deep, commanding voice.

'Mirandi? Mirandi, are you in there? Sweetheart, are you all right?'

Her heart boomeranged around her chest cavity and she sprang up out of the bed. 'Oh…' She started a wild run for the door, but bumped into an armoire and stubbed her toe on the dressing table. Catching sight of herself in the wing mirrors, she shrieked, 'Oh, no.'

Limping and running, she made it to the front door without bouncing off any other pieces of furniture, and halted there. 'Joe? Is that you?'

'Of course it's me.' He sounded slightly bewildered by the question. 'Who else?'

'Can you give me a minute?'

There was an incredulous silence, then she felt sure she heard him sigh.

'A minute. Fine. All right.'

She turned for the bathroom, remembered she couldn't go in there, and made for the kitchen sink instead. Forget hygiene. This was an emergency. She splashed her face and dried it on a tea towel, then hurried back to the bedroom to do her best with make-up.

Transformed to some degree, a minute or so later she opened the door. Well, all right, it might have been several minutes.

Joe was slouched against the wall in the hallway with his eyes shut.

'Hello,' she said, hoping she didn't still sound bleary. 'Sorry to keep you.'

He opened his eyes and sprang to his feet, and his eyes lit up.

They truly did.

Before another word was spoken he grabbed her and dragged her against his lean sexy bones in the most comprehensive embrace, showering her with kisses and growling things like, 'Oh, I've missed you. Oh, it's been so *hard*. Oh, to feel you. To *hold* you. I've needed this. You'll never *know*.'

Her heart spilling over with joy and relief, she didn't attempt to discourage his flattering words, but when he walked her backwards into the flat and directed her with an unerring instinct towards her bedroom she felt it was time to draw a line in the sand.

'It's good to see you too,' she panted. 'I thought you weren't coming back.'

'I know you thought that,' he said with a hearty laugh. 'Your emails were full of it.'

She raised a brow at that. As far as she knew her emails had been models of restraint. 'Well, but… What did you expect? How did you think I would feel? What's all this about you resigning?'

He made an exasperated, '*Tsk*. Who told you that? I bet it

was Ryan Patterson. It was supposed to be top secret until I had everything tied up.'

'Well, didn't you think I might be *interested*?'

'Of course I did, sweetheart, of course, but…' They'd reached her bedroom by this time, and he steered her towards the only surface where someone might sit, which was the bed. Her rather rumpled bed.

He didn't appear to notice that, though. It seemed he only had eyes for her. He gazed tenderly at her and softened his voice as if she were an invalid. 'Well, sweetheart, I know how you worry and I wanted to tell you face to face. I gathered you were feeling a little down and I thought it might upset you if you heard the news without knowing the full story.'

Hope rose in her heart. 'What *is* the full story?'

He sprang up and started striding about and flinging his arms about as he talked. 'Well, in the first place it was about this *firm*. I haven't always been happy with the direction things were taking.' He halted to look at her, the light of excitement blazing in his eyes. 'I've been feeling restless for some time. You know, some of the things the board are so keen to support aren't really my thing. So I've decided to start my own firm.'

'Wow.' She widened her eyes. 'Well, *that* sounds good.'

Smiling, he sat down beside her. 'I knew you'd be right there with me. *I* feel pretty good about it. I emailed my resignation to give them time to digest it before I came back. Some members of the board have already tried to talk me out of it, but I think this is the right time to make the break. I feel as if everything has come together for me at this point in my life. Do you know that feeling?'

Her heart skipped a massive beat. 'Well…'

He seized her hands in his strong, warm grasp. 'I'm not sure if this change started with my having to go to Monte Carlo, or with finding *you* again, but it's all worked together and it's been the most *special* time. Honestly, my darling girl, I feel as if I'm floating on air. And without you, none of it would have happened.'

He kissed her so deeply and tenderly she nearly swooned. It had been *so long*. And all the time she was thinking—my darling girl? She was still his darling girl? Her heart began to thrill with the most fantastic instinct. Could it be…?

'Oh,' she said at last after she'd gasped in some air. 'Of course it would all have happened. You'd have still gone to Monte Carlo and found out the real truth about who you are. And I know you'd have gone to see Amelie in the end.'

His face became grave. 'Possibly, and all of those things were important, of course. But the most important was *us*. Don't you think?'

She nodded for seconds, unable to prevent herself from beaming, and, after all she'd done to try to reclaim them, her eyes filled up with more tears. 'I do think so. Yes, Joe, I do.'

She noticed then that Joe's eyes had that shimmer she'd only seen once before, the day in Antibes, and her heart surged with love and tenderness for him.

'I wanted to tell you so many times while we were away.' His voice was serious, his stunning eyes alight with a sincere, ardent glow. 'But there always seemed to be so much going on, the moment didn't arrive. So I'll try to say it now. I love you, Mirandi. You're the only one for me. I—love you so much I don't ever want to be without you again.'

She felt as if pure, incandescent joy must shine from her. 'And I love you, my darling Joe,' she breathed. 'I've always loved you.'

'Really?' To her absolute amazement, he got off the bed and onto his knees. She stared at him, fascinated. Then he said, 'Well, then, Mirandi… Will you—will you marry me?'

Her most precious, solemn moment had arrived and she felt composed solely of starbursts and ecstasy and bubbling, hilarious laughter. 'Oh, yes, *yes*! I'll marry you.'

She couldn't help giggling as he got up off the floor, but

he grabbed her to him then with such masculine conviction, kissing her back against the pillows, that she was stirred with nothing but the gravest respect.

She was just settling into position for some fantastic and overdue pre-marital bliss when Joe raised his head and interrupted his passionate appreciation of her. 'Er…excuse me a second. I've only just got off the plane. Customs, you know. And then there was the wait in the hall. Where's the bathroom here?'

She sighed. 'It's just through there and down that hall.'

'Won't be a second.' As he strode off in the direction of the bathroom a shocking thought struck her.

'*Joe.*'

She bounded from the bed and raced to catch up with him. Cutting him off, she darted in front of him in the nick of time and stood with her back to the door.

'Joe, you can't go in there.'

He looked thoroughly bemused. 'I can't? Why not?'

She gazed at him for seconds while a million complex thoughts scrambled to make sense of themselves inside her mushy brain.

His black brows merged together in total perplexity. 'Why not, Mirandi? What is it?' His tone grew demanding. 'What's—*who's* in that bathroom?'

She let out a long breath. 'Well, Joe…my darling Joe.' She smiled and trailed her fingers up his gorgeous arms and clung to them as tightly as she could. 'You see…as it happens… there's something I may have to tell you.'

Harlequin *Presents*

Coming Next Month

from **Harlequin Presents®**. Available June 28, 2011.

#2999 A STORMY SPANISH SUMMER
Penny Jordan

#3000 A NIGHT OF SCANDAL
Sarah Morgan
The Notorious Wolfes

#3001 AFTER THEIR VOWS
Michelle Reid

#3002 THE WEDDING CHARADE
Melanie Milburne
The Sabbatini Brothers

#3003 ALESSANDRO'S PRIZE
Helen Bianchin

#3004 THE ULTIMATE RISK
Chantelle Shaw

Coming Next Month

from **Harlequin Presents®** EXTRA. Available July 12, 2011.

#157 A SPANISH AWAKENING
Kim Lawrence
One Night in…

#158 RECKLESS NIGHT IN RIO
Jennie Lucas
One Night in…

#159 THE END OF FAKING IT
Natalie Anderson
His Very Personal Assistant

#160 HER NOT-SO-SECRET DIARY
Anne Oliver
His Very Personal Assistant

REQUEST YOUR FREE BOOKS!

◆Harlequin *Presents*

2 FREE NOVELS PLUS
2 FREE GIFTS!

PASSION
GUARANTEED
SEDUCTION

YES! Please send me 2 FREE Harlequin Presents® novels and my 2 FREE gifts (gifts are worth about $10). After receiving them, if I don't wish to receive any more books, I can return the shipping statement marked "cancel." If I don't cancel, I will receive 6 brand-new novels every month and be billed just $4.05 per book in the U.S. or $4.74 per book in Canada. That's a saving of at least 15% off the cover price! It's quite a bargain! Shipping and handling is just 50¢ per book in the U.S. and 75¢ per book in Canada.* I understand that accepting the 2 free books and gifts places me under no obligation to buy anything. I can always return a shipment and cancel at any time. Even if I never buy another book, the two free books and gifts are mine to keep forever.

106/306 HDN FC55

Name _____ (PLEASE PRINT)

Address _____ Apt. #

City _____ State/Prov. _____ Zip/Postal Code

Signature (if under 18, a parent or guardian must sign)

Mail to the **Reader Service:**
IN U.S.A.: P.O. Box 1867, Buffalo, NY 14240-1867
IN CANADA: P.O. Box 609, Fort Erie, Ontario L2A 5X3

Not valid for current subscribers to Harlequin Presents books.

**Are you a current subscriber to Harlequin Presents books
and want to receive the larger-print edition?
Call 1-800-873-8635 or visit www.ReaderService.com.**

* Terms and prices subject to change without notice. Prices do not include applicable taxes. Sales tax applicable in N.Y. Canadian residents will be charged applicable taxes. Offer not valid in Quebec. This offer is limited to one order per household. All orders subject to credit approval. Credit or debit balances in a customer's account(s) may be offset by any other outstanding balance owed by or to the customer. Please allow 4 to 6 weeks for delivery. Offer available while quantities last.

Your Privacy—The Reader Service is committed to protecting your privacy. Our Privacy Policy is available online at www.ReaderService.com or upon request from the Reader Service.

We make a portion of our mailing list available to reputable third parties that offer products we believe may interest you. If you prefer that we not exchange your name with third parties, or if you wish to clarify or modify your communication preferences, please visit us at www.ReaderService.com/consumerschoice or write to us at Reader Service Preference Service, P.O. Box 9062, Buffalo, NY 14269. Include your complete name and address.

USA TODAY *bestselling author B.J. Daniels*
takes you on a trip to Whitehorse, Montana,
and the Chisholm Cattle Company.

RUSTLED

Available July 2011 from Harlequin Intrigue.

As the dust settled, Dawson got his first good look at the rustler. A pair of big Montana sky-blue eyes glared up at him from a face framed by blond curls.

A woman rustler?

"You have to let me go," she hollered as the roar of the stampeding cattle died off in the distance.

"So you can finish stealing my cattle? I don't think so." Dawson jerked the woman to her feet.

She reached for the gun strapped to her hip hidden under her long barn jacket.

He grabbed the weapon before she could, his eyes narrowing as he assessed her. "How many others are there?" he demanded, grabbing a fistful of her jacket. "I think you'd better start talking before I tear into you."

She tried to fight him off, but he was on to her tricks and pinned her to the ground. He was suddenly aware of the soft curves beneath the jean jacket she wore under her coat.

"You have to listen to me." She ground out the words from between her gritted teeth. "You have to let me go. If you don't they will come back for me and they will kill you. There are too many of them for you to fight off alone. You won't stand a chance and I don't want your blood on my hands."

"I'm touched by your concern for me. Especially after you just tried to pull a gun on me."

"I wasn't going to shoot you."

Dawson hauled her to her feet and walked her the rest of the way to his horse. Reaching into his saddlebag, he pulled out a length of rope.

"You can't tie me up."

He pulled her hands behind her back and began to tie her wrists together.

"If you let me go, I can keep them from coming back," she said. "You have my word." She let out an unladylike curse. "I'm just trying to save your sorry neck."

"And I'm just going after my cattle."

"Don't you mean your boss's cattle?"

"Those cattle are mine."

"*You're* a Chisholm?"

"Dawson Chisholm. And you are…?"

"Everyone calls me Jinx."

He chuckled. "I can see why."

Bronco busting, falling in love…it's all in a day's work.
Look for the rest of their story in

RUSTLED

Available July 2011 from Harlequin Intrigue
wherever books are sold.